THE HOUSE NEXT DOOR

THE HOUSE NEXT DOOR

RICHIE TANKERSLEY CUSICK

SIMON PULSE
New York London Toronto Sydney Singapore

This book is a work of fiction. Any references to historical events, real people, or real locales are used fictitiously. Other names, characters, places, and incidents are the product of the author's imagination, and any resemblance to actual events or locales or persons, living or dead, is entirely coincidental.

First Simon Pulse edition January 2002
Text copyright © 2002 by Richie Tankersley Cusick

SIMON PULSE
An imprint of Simon & Schuster
Children's Publishing Division
1230 Avenue of the Americas
New York, NY 10020

The text of this book was set in Exlibris.

Printed in the United States of America

2 4 6 8 10 9 7 5 3 1

Library of Congress Control Number: 2001096345

ISBN 0-7434-1838-7

To Mary
For teaching me how to
Drive in the snow,
Be fashionably late,
Love kitties,
Use attractive skillets,
And for teaching me everything
I know about writing.

THE HOUSE NEXT DOOR

1

"You've decided *what?*" Emma demanded. "Have you lost your mind?"

"I haven't lost my mind, and I think it's a great idea," Val told her. "Our next English assignment's to write about something strange or scary, right? So I've decided to write about you and Charlie."

For a moment Emma forgot the notebooks, papers, and junk food piled around her at the foot of the bed. Instead she gazed over at her best friend and groaned.

"Val, please tell me you're kidding. And please tell me Charlie's the scary one."

Val's face brightened. "I'm not kidding. Everyone's fascinated by twins—the bond between them, the way they communicate—"

"He yells 'Hey, stupid!' That's how Charlie communicates with me."

"Very funny. Come on, it's a great idea! And since I know you both so well, I won't feel weird interviewing you. It can be an in-depth, sensitive, soul-searching kind of thing."

"Charlie has no depth." Frowning, Emma considered the matter, then shook her head. "The soul part I'm not so sure about, but you can definitely rule out sensitive."

Val leaned one hip against the vanity table and carefully inspected her chartreuse fingernails. "This is me ignoring you. In the meantime, I have three weeks to come up with some fantastically brilliant questions."

"Okay, here's one. How about the probability that my *real* twin and I were separated at birth, and someone left Charlie on our doorstep as a bad joke?"

"Not exactly what I had in mind." Val frowned. "And is that the last brownie I see you eating?"

Emma's hand froze halfway to her mouth. Sheepishly she lowered the brownie, broke off a section, and held it in Val's direction.

"I thought you said these were terrible," she defended herself as Val snatched it away.

"They are, but I'm totally stressed out. God, Emma, I don't know why you even try doing homemade—why don't you just use a mix?"

"This *is* a mix."

"That's so pathetic." Val swallowed the brownie and promptly made a face. "Okay, listen. Questions can really make or break an interview, you know. Remember when I interviewed that medium for the school paper, and I asked her all that stuff about séances, and then I won that journalism award—"

"And then she turned out later to be a big fake?" Emma reminded her.

"Thank you very much. The fact remains, I still did a great interview! And my paper on you and Charlie will be a—a masterpiece!"

Sighing, Emma ran a hand back through her short blond hair. Just the thought of having her private life exposed made her cringe. Not to mention how Charlie would react at being linked to her in any way, shape, or form—twins or not.

"Look, just forget about Charlie and me," she urged. "Write about something else that's strange or scary. Something *interesting*."

Val looked indignant. "Well, I can't write about what *really* scares me, can I? Do you really think Mr. Hoffman's going to give me an A for 'What If Nobody Invites Me to the Winter Dance'?"

"Someone'll ask you. Someone *always* asks you."

"Yeah, but the someones who usually ask me and the someone—I mean, someones—I *wish* would ask me are *very different* someones!"

"Any someones I might know?" Emma mentioned casually, but Val didn't seem to hear. Instead she caught her long black hair in an upsweep and began twirling the length of the room.

"It's all Roger's fault anyway," Val declared.

"How's that?"

"He invited me months and months ago, then his family decided to move away!"

"The nerve of him." Hiding a smile, Emma adjusted

one cuff of her crocheted sweater. "So just go alone, if nobody asks you."

"I'd be completely mortified."

"You can go with me. I don't have a date."

"You never do."

"Ouch. Are we feeling a little mean?"

Val pirouetted to a stop, instantly contrite.

"That's not what I meant. I just meant that if any of the guys from school asked you, you *know* you wouldn't go."

"Why wouldn't I?"

"You're much too particular. It's a well-known fact."

In spite of their joking, Emma felt herself bristle.

"Well, I might go!" she insisted. "And what's so bad about being particular? I'd love to have a boyfriend. So why shouldn't I hold out for what I really want?"

"Because the guy you really want could never exist in real life," Val chided. "You've told me about your dream guy a million times. Your tall, dark, handsome hero. *Nobody* could be that perfect. And not to change the subject, but when are we going to fix up this bedroom? It's plain, it's dark—"

"You *are* changing the subject, and no matter how good you are at it, our test is still tomorrow, so could you please concentrate on English lit for maybe two whole seconds?"

"I'll never use it when I become a supermodel-actress."

"Not even to star in a blockbuster film that's based on some Jane Austen novel?"

"It's completely old-fashioned, Em. Your room, I mean, not English lit, although—"

"I like old-fashioned."

"This furniture is ugly—"

"Antique," Emma corrected her. Her blue eyes made a quick, satisfied sweep of the room, from the four-poster bed to the skirted dressing table to the pale flowery wallpaper that had certainly seen better days. "Antique," she repeated, her gaze returning to Val. "It belonged to some great-great—who-knows-how-great aunt on my mom's side, and I like it. It makes me feel like I'm in a . . . a sweeter time."

Val turned to Emma and raised a critical eyebrow. "*Sweeter time?* What does that mean, exactly—sweeter time? Dull, maybe. Sweet, no. You know, despite my best efforts to corrupt you, you are still way too serious. I'm beginning to feel like a total failure!"

"It's my job to be serious. *Somebody* has to keep you in line."

Emma settled herself more comfortably with her notebooks, unwrapped a candy bar, then glanced up again as Val sashayed past the bed and over to the window.

"Now what're you doing?" she asked.

Val lifted the shade and peered out into the night.

"I bet I know what you're doing *your* English paper on," she said softly. "The strange and scary house next door . . . where ghosts and ghouls stare in at Emma Donovan. . . ."

Emma felt her nerves tighten, but she did her best to sound indifferent. "You mean the old Farmington place? Why would I want to write about that?"

"Because it's creepy and spooky, and the whole thing should be torn down."

"This whole neighborhood should be torn down." Emma sighed. "Current residence included."

Val cast her a sympathetic glance. "Well, at least this isn't as bad as the crazy Miss Lobergs' house. They must have been *born* in that house—they've been there forever."

Emma nodded agreement. The two spinster sisters lived on the opposite end of the neighborhood and had long been a part of local folklore.

"You remember that time I tried to turn my car around in their driveway"—Val giggled—"and the tall one came flying off the porch throwing rocks at me?"

"You were dressed like a giant shamrock, for God's sake. And it wasn't rocks, it was peanuts. She was out there feeding her squirrels when you showed up. You're lucky you didn't give her a heart attack."

Val looked offended. "It was St. Patrick's Day! And anyway, I won first prize for the most original costume."

"Miss Loberg thought you were pretty original, all right."

"Well, I don't care what you say," Val insisted. "Those two old ladies are crazy."

"Eccentric," Emma corrected her again.

"They kill stray animals and eat little children for breakfast. Everyone says so."

"Everyone who?" Emma asked, but Val rushed on.

"This area's not safe anymore. I wish you guys would move."

Emma wished so, too. The entire neighborhood was sad and rundown—one of the oldest in Hartville—but ever since Emma's father died, there hadn't been enough money even to consider moving anywhere else.

Val, on the other hand, lived on the west side of town—"Posh Park," as all their friends called it—with her own car and credit cards, a swimming pool, and a housekeeper. Val was the only child of two prominent surgeons; Emma's mom was a night-shift nurse at the hospital. Val had vacationed in Europe seventeen times; Emma had lived her whole life within a three-hundred-mile radius. Yet despite such different backgrounds and upbringings, something special had clicked between the two girls that very first week of high school.

Emma smiled now, remembering.

She and Charlie had just moved to town, and while Charlie had been an instant hit with guys and girls alike, Emma had felt awkward and isolated in her new surroundings. She'd been sitting alone at lunch one day when Val approached her, all hot-pink suede and self-confident swagger.

"Hey! New girl!" She'd sat down without an invitation and promptly helped herself to half of Emma's sandwich. "You *are* new, right?"

Startled, Emma had managed a nod.

"Yeah, well, being new sucks big time, let me tell you." Val had grabbed her hand and shaken it. "I'm Val. Also new in Hartville. Daughter of Mr. Just-Appointed-Head-Honcho at the hospital—that's director of Hartville General to you—which means I've been kidnapped and brought here kicking and screaming against my will. I don't know a soul—which doesn't bother me in the least—but these girls around here all think they're *more* than special—which they're most definitely not—and there seems to be some pathetic little rule about not letting new girls into any of these pathetic little cliques. So this is how I figure it. You and I can be our *own* clique. And then *they* can be the outsiders. What do you say?"

That had been nearly four years ago. And though Emma had eventually made friends and Val was by far the most popular girl in school, the two of them had remained close.

"Em, are you even listening to me?"

With a start, Emma turned her attention back to the window. Val was gazing outside again, her voice lowered to a shivery whisper.

"See how it just sits there and watches us? Like some big old corpse? Come over here and look."

"Oh, for heaven's sakes." With a bravado she didn't really feel, Emma got up and marched across the room. She stopped behind Val, and together they stared out into the darkness.

Pale moonlight flickered behind a bank of ragged clouds, throwing the Farmington house in and out of shadow. A raw November wind scraped dead leaves along the deserted driveway below.

From here they could see over the fence and across the wide expanse of property next door, across the deep patches of overgrown weeds and wild, tangled shrubbery that rendered the house practically invisible from the street. Clumps of ivy and drooping oaks overhung its chimneys and porches. Once-white Victorian walls had weathered to an ashen gray, and broken gingerbread trim hung from the eaves like scabs. The three-story Farmington house sat there on its huge lot, far back and all alone, completely enclosed by a high, spiked, wrought-iron fence. Its second-floor windows were clearly visible from Emma's room, and all of them were shrouded in tattered lace curtains.

Emma always felt cold when she looked at that house—bone-deep cold even on the hottest day and surrounded by people. It was as though some primal instinct always roused inside of her, calling her, yet warning her at the same time. She'd tried to explain it once to Charlie and Val, but they'd teased her so unmercifully that she'd never mentioned it again. Not that they'd ever forget it, she thought ruefully, or let *her* forget it.

"Okay, Val." Pulling back from the window, Emma tried to keep her voice steady. "Enough ghost stories for one night."

But Val's dark eyes had a mischievous twinkle. "Do you think it's really haunted? Like everyone says?"

Before Emma could answer, Val turned back to the window, propping her elbows on the sill, peering out once more into the night.

Emma sat down on the bed. With grim determination she picked up some papers and began sorting through them.

"Okay, Val, I'll quiz you first. Let's do the romantic poets and the influence they had on—"

"Oh, God," Val said softly.

For a second Emma was confused. She skimmed the paper in front of her and frowned.

"No, that's not right. Mr. Hoffman said we wouldn't go into any religious aspects of—"

"Someone's there, Em. In the house."

Emma looked up. She could see Val standing ramrod straight, her fingers gripping the edge of the windowsill.

She could hear the trembling in her voice.

"Someone's watching us, Emma."

For another brief second Emma hesitated. Then she forced a laugh.

"Come on, Val, stop playing around. It's getting late, and we're not even halfway done."

"I'm not joking." Without taking her eyes from the windowpane, Val motioned her friend to come closer. "Look. There—in that window."

Emma didn't want to look. Her body felt weighted down, and there was an odd pounding in the back of her head.

"Turn off the light," Val said.

Emma nodded. She touched the lightswitch, plunging the room into darkness. She crept over to Val's side and swept her gaze across the house next door.

"See it?" Val nudged her. "Please tell me you see it."

A shiver crawled up Emma's spine.

"I . . ."

Her voice seemed to freeze in her throat. She was vaguely aware that she and Val were clutching hands.

It was more like a shadow, really—a dark, misshapen silhouette framed in a window on the second floor. It hovered there behind torn lace curtains, but Emma was absolutely certain now that it was watching them.

She could feel the eyes.

A gaze so piercing, so intense, that it chilled her very soul.

2

⚜

"That thing," Val whispered. "What is it?"

Emma shook her head. A sudden draft swept through the room, and without warning, a hand came out of the darkness, sliding over her shoulder.

Emma shrieked. As she jumped and knocked Val off balance, both girls fell in a heap on the floor, yelling at the top of their lungs.

The light snapped on. A tall figure stared down at them with a grin.

"*Charlie!*" Emma shouted furiously. "What are you *doing?*"

She ignored the hand he reached out to her. Instead she got clumsily to her feet and began to advance on him.

"You could have given us both heart attacks! What's *wrong* with you?"

Her twin brother took a step back, his grin widening.

"What's wrong with *me*?" he echoed. "What are you two doing holding hands here in the dark?"

Val rose in one graceful movement. She gave Charlie the fiercest look she could muster, then quickly turned back to the window.

"I don't see anything now," she said.

"See what?" Charlie asked.

"Oh, Emma thought she saw something at that window over there," Val told him, poker-faced.

Charlie raised an eyebrow and looked from one girl to the other. "Oh, sorry. If I'd known you were that much into the window-peeping thing—"

"Me!" Emma's voice went shrill. "Val's the one who saw it first!"

For a moment Val stared at her in utter amazement. "*I* saw something? What do you mean, *I* saw something?" She turned to Charlie and sighed. "I swear, Charlie, I don't know what she's talking about!"

"That shadow!" Emma yelped. "It was clear as day!"

"Shadows aren't clear, Em," Charlie retorted. "That's why they're called . . . you know . . . shadows."

Emma glared at him as Val burst out laughing.

"Oh, Emma, I couldn't resist!" Val grabbed her friend and gave her an enormous hug. "You're just so much fun to pick on!"

Flustered, Emma disentangled herself from Val's arms. She could hear Charlie laughing, too, in the background, and along with that dull pounding in her head, her body felt strangely numb.

A joke?

As her thoughts whirled, Emma tried to clutch at

some shred of reality. So Val had only *pretended* to see someone in the window next door. There hadn't really been anyone there at all—only a shadow—a normal nighttime shadow and Emma's own crazy imagination. *I should've known better,* she scolded herself. *I should've known Val was teasing, that she and Charlie would just gang up on me, except—*

She bit her lip in confusion.

Except it wasn't just a shadow. I saw something . . . someone! I know somebody was there. . . .

"Way to go, Em." Charlie winked. "Welcome once again to the Gullible Hall of Fame."

Recovering herself, she gave him a shove toward the door. "Get out. Can't you see we're trying to study?"

"In the dark. Right."

"I mean it, Charlie! That wasn't the least bit funny."

"Now, Em, you have to admit. It was a *little* funny."

"Close the door behind you."

"I don't know why you always start something you can't finish." He sighed, easily grabbing both her hands in his. "You know you'll just end up getting hurt."

"*Out!*"

As usual with Charlie, Emma couldn't decide whether to laugh or to scream. No one could make her crazy the way Charlie could. No one could try her patience more, make her as furious, or make her sides hurt from laughing like Charlie could.

And nobody knew her so well.

Despite their obvious gender differences, the resemblance between them was startling. Same tall, thin build, high cheekbones, and delicate features; same silky blond hair and deep blue eyes—except that Charlie stood three inches higher than his sister and wore his hair six inches longer.

Every girl at Hartville High was in love with Charlie Donovan.

Emma knew this for a fact, and was completely mystified by it. From what she'd been able to learn from the general female populace, it wasn't just his great looks and laid-back manner that captivated them, but some perfect blending of intelligence and modesty, humor and sweetness—not to mention a touch of endearing shyness—that caused them all to find Charlie so irresistible. Frankly, Emma didn't see what all the fuss was about. She knew how her brother acted in front of the world—but she also knew those insecure and really annoying private sides to him that the rest of the world would never see. She also knew that Val had a huge crush on Charlie—had for about two years now. It was a point of pride with Val that she'd managed to hide it from everyone—especially Emma—for so long; a point of honor with Emma that she'd managed to play along so well. Though what Val possibly saw in her brother she couldn't begin to understand.

Now, as she wrestled Charlie into the hallway, Emma threw out a parting shot.

"You'd both feel pretty stupid if there really *was* something next door! Maybe you shouldn't make fun of that house!"

"We're not making fun of the house," Charlie countered. "We're making fun of you." Releasing her suddenly, he sent Emma sprawling on the end of the bed.

Val walked over to help her up. "Come on, Em, I'm

sorry. Let's just forget about it and concentrate on—"

"I *saw* something," Emma insisted stubbornly, but Charlie just rolled his eyes.

"You probably saw my car lights when I turned in the driveway."

"They wouldn't show up that high or that far." Emma scowled, rubbing her wrists. "Maybe someone broke in. Maybe someone's staying over there."

"What, some bum?" Charlie shook his head. "I doubt it. Don't you think we'd have seen something suspicious? I mean, he'd have to go out for food or find a bathroom somewhere. None of the utilities are on— no heat or water."

Val was beginning to look sheepish. "You're not going to have nightmares about this all night, are you?"

"No, but she'll probably flunk that English test tomorrow." A slow smile spread over Charlie's lips. "Thanks for traumatizing her, moron."

"Will you just *go*?" Emma marched to the door and slammed it. Then she turned back and frowned at Val.

"Look, maybe you really did think you saw something," Val soothed. She watched as Emma crossed to the window and stared out. "It *could* have been Charlie's headlights. Or the moon behind a cloud. It could have been *anything*. A nice, normal anything."

"Or my imagination," Emma grumbled, lowering the shade. "That's what you're really thinking."

She put one hand to her forehead, as though she could press the awful memory away. That eerie sensation of being watched . . . the soul-chilling intensity of those invisible eyes . . .

"Nobody's there, Emma," Val said firmly, and Emma gave her a reluctant nod.

Of course Val was right; the house next door was empty.

And old empty houses were nothing to be afraid of.

3

Charlie couldn't stop thinking about the house.

He couldn't stop thinking about the house next door, and it was really starting to annoy him.

He punched his pillow and wadded it up, and then he wrapped the whole thing around his head.

"Jeez, Emma, what's going on with you anyway?" he muttered.

Because at some instinctive level, he knew these thoughts belonged to his sister and not to him. He'd lived with Emma his whole life, lived with this creepy psychic bond they both shared, and he could recognize immediately when certain thoughts were his and when they were his twin's. "Stop it," he ordered them now.

He tried to shut them out. Just like all the countless other times he managed to shut out Emma's dramatic highs and lows, all her stupid neuroses. Only tonight it wasn't working. He hadn't been bombarded by her thoughts like this in . . . well, he couldn't remember *how* long it had been since an onslaught this intense.

Groaning, he flopped over in bed and reached for the clock on the nightstand. Three A.M.

"So get a grip already," he begged her. "Some of us are trying to sleep."

The image of the Farmington house faded.

Charlie could feel his heart begin to race, could feel his breath quicken in his throat. He closed his eyes and for a brief instant, gave in to the turmoil in his head—shadows . . . ghostly images . . . nothing substantial except the depth of emotional confusion, sharp and cutting as physical pain. A level so deep, it could only be one of dreams. And nightmares . . .

"Come on, Em . . . wake up . . ."

He reminded himself that after seventeen years he should be used to sudden attacks of Emma's most extreme thoughts and feelings—even dreams—when he least expected it. Emma had always been a lot moodier than he was, a whole lot more unpredictable, and he couldn't keep his mental guard up against her every single minute of the day and night. Still, he usually excelled at being able to block her out—and hiding his own thoughts from her—when he really tried; it was a technique he'd started honing when they were just children. "Self-defense," he loved to tease her, "against your weirdness." Of course, it made Emma absolutely furious when he did it. And if their mental battle waged too fiercely, he could expect to pay a high price for it afterward. A splitting headache, sometimes nausea or brief disorientation, and always a body that felt totally drained.

He was beginning to feel the effects even now.

"Dammit, Emma!" Charlie yelled. "Cut it out!"

He wanted to get out of bed, but the room was spinning around him. He closed his eyes and gripped the mattress with both hands. He could feel his mind giving way as a torrent of emotions rushed through him, and he had no choice but to ride the surge like a runaway roller coaster.

In true brotherly fashion, he tried to comfort himself by imagining all the ways he'd get back at Emma tomorrow.

"*If* I live through this," he told himself grimly.

He yanked the covers over his head and groaned louder.

It was going to be a long night.

4

"Oh. Are you addressing me?" Emma frowned at her brother across the kitchen table. "I'm sorry. I'm afraid I didn't hear anything worth listening to."

Scowling, Charlie slid farther down in his chair. "I hope you flunk your English test," he grumbled for the second time. He rubbed his forehead, winced, then pushed his plate of scrambled eggs away.

"What's wrong?" Mrs. Donovan asked. She'd just gotten home from her all-night job, but she always insisted on the three of them having breakfast together. Now she ruffled Charlie's hair affectionately and prodded him to sit up straight. "Didn't you sleep well?"

"No," he muttered. "Thanks to Emma."

Emma wasn't in the mood for arguing this morning. She'd tossed and turned all night, thinking about the Farmington house, and when she'd finally dozed off in the early hours of the morning, her dreams had been full of phantoms.

"Fine," she muttered back. "I hope you were miserable all night."

Amused, their mother glanced at each of them in turn. "Sounds like you two have been trespassing on each other's sleep again."

"He's the trespasser," Emma said. "They're *my* dreams."

"Why don't you dream about something interesting?" Charlie complained. "Like naked girls or something."

Mrs. Donovan laughed and popped more bread into the toaster. "You know, if I had a dollar for every single time we've discussed this over the years—"

"You'd be a very rich woman," Charlie and Emma finished blandly.

Their mother laughed again. "Yes, I would! A millionaire at the very least!"

Despite her sour mood, Emma couldn't help smiling. Poor Mom . . . she'd been looking so tired lately, but somehow she always managed to keep a positive outlook. Emma knew her mother worried about money, that she wished they could all move to a nicer house; she knew Mom had taken on a tough schedule at the hospital, not only because it paid better, but mostly because she wanted to be there for her kids when they got up every morning and when they got home from school every afternoon. To her and Charlie's distress, Mom had refused to let them take part-time jobs during the school year. "Studies come first," she'd insist. "And once you're out in the world, you'll have the rest of your lives to work."

"So . . ." Mom's cheery voice brought Emma back to the present. "Do we want to talk about what happened last night? Would it help?"

"She's beyond help," Charlie stated. "It's sad. But it's true."

Emma ignored him. "I couldn't sleep, that's all. And when I finally did, I had all these nightmares."

"About what?" her mother urged, but Emma frowned again.

"I don't know. There might've been ghosts. I can't remember."

Charlie gave a snort as his mother turned to him.

"How about you, Charlie? Did you see anything?"

"Not really." Charlie shook his head. "Mostly just a bunch of weird feelings—really intense. My heart kept racing, and my thoughts wouldn't keep still."

"Any *specific* thoughts?"

"No. Dizzy. Everything went so fast, I felt sick."

"Then why didn't you just tune me out?" Emma's smile was saccharine-sweet as Charlie mimicked one back at her.

"Don't think I didn't try."

"Aren't you ashamed, Emma?" Mom gave her a sly wink. "Giving your brother such a terrible headache?"

Emma couldn't have looked less repentant. "He did it himself. Anyway, I hate when he tries to shut me out. It's like pushing against a brick wall."

"Is that why you ambushed me while I was sleeping?" Charlie threw back. "When all my defenses were down?"

The twins stared at each other. It was always like

this—*had* always been like this, ever since they were born—this weird psychic connection they shared. When Emma was small, she'd thought *all* brothers and sisters were like she and Charlie, that all siblings could feel each other's feelings and read each other's thoughts and invade each other's dreams. She'd been amazed to learn that she and Charlie were different from most people—"special," their mom insisted. Mom had always accepted their closeness and encouraged them to see it for the extraordinary gift it was—a bond that no one else in the world could ever be a part of.

Emma had never quite understood it herself, this bond, this mysterious ability to hear and see and sense certain things that one's twin was experiencing at the very same time. It had been a source of fun when they were children, an increasing source of annoyance as they'd grown up, and she'd always felt a little jealous that Charlie seemed better at it than she was. Eventually the two had learned to put up guards against each other—temporary mental blocks to keep the other one at bay. But here again, Charlie seemed the more skillful, and it frustrated Emma like crazy when he deliberately shut her out.

"I didn't ambush you," Emma told him now. "I was minding my own business."

Mrs. Donovan set some jam on the table. She slid Charlie's plate back in front of him, then glanced thoughtfully at her daughter.

"Emma," she suggested, "maybe you really *were* trying to communicate with Charlie. Something you weren't even consciously aware of . . . something you might have needed him for."

The twins exchanged glances. Emma looked pained.

"Mom. Think about it. Why would anyone ever need Charlie for anything?"

Before Charlie could answer, his mother rushed on. "Well, something was obviously bothering you," she told Emma. "I wish you could remember what it was. And it's too bad Charlie wasn't more receptive to it."

"Oh, sure." Charlie sighed. "Blame it on me. Hey, I don't need sleep . . . I don't need privacy–"

"Well, it's not like I want you reading all my most personal thoughts, either," Emma broke in.

"Like any of them could possibly be worth reading."

Emma threw her toast at him. It landed on his plate, and Charlie calmly picked it up and began eating.

"Okay, you two." Sitting down at the table, Mrs. Donovan tactfully changed the subject. "What's on the agenda today?"

"English test," Emma mumbled.

"Which she's gonna flunk," Charlie added.

"And a committee meeting for the winter dance," Emma reminded him. "So I won't be riding home with you this afternoon."

Charlie smiled toward the heavens. "Aah! There *is* a God!"

"And when's the dance?" their mother asked. "Do you two have dates?"

Emma made a face. "Why are you even bringing that up?"

"What about you, heartthrob?" Mrs. Donovan teased.

Her son's shoulders moved in a shrug. "I don't know. I haven't decided yet."

"You're really unbelievable." Emma sounded mildly

disgusted. "Every girl in the whole school would die to go out with you—do *not* ask me why—and you still haven't called anyone? The dance is only a few weeks away!"

Another shrug.

"Why don't you ask Val?" Emma suggested, leaning toward him.

Charlie's mouth dropped open. "What? Are you out of your mind?"

"Well, why not? Roger won't be taking her now, and she needs a date."

"Yeah, like I'm that desperate."

"She'd go. She's been in love with you forever."

This time Charlie looked genuinely shocked. Emma watched closely as he tried to recover himself.

"You're crazy," he muttered.

"She has."

"Oh, yeah?" Charlie squirmed uncomfortably in his chair. "And I guess she told you that?"

"She'd never tell me that. She tries to hide it from me all the time. But I just know."

Charlie had an odd look on his face. For a split second his control slipped, and Emma felt an unexpected jumble of confusion, pleasure, and embarrassment before his mental wall snapped firmly into place. She gave a sly smile as he took another bite of toast.

"Right," he snorted, talking with his mouth full. "And you and she are—correct me if I'm wrong here—best friends?"

Emma kept smiling.

"Who tell each other *everything*? Everything in the *world*?"

Emma glanced at her mother, who was obviously

enjoying Charlie's predicament. "That's what best friends do," Emma agreed innocently. "So why don't you ask Val out?"

"Why don't you? You were the one holding hands with her last night."

"But she'd much rather hold yours."

Now Mrs. Donovan couldn't help joining in. "Come on, Charlie, why not? I think it's a wonderful idea."

"You'd have this huge advantage," Emma persisted. "I mean, you've known each other for a long time, so it's not like you wouldn't have anything to talk about."

Charlie was looking at her as though she had snakes growing out of her hair.

"And besides, she wants to interview you for an English project," Emma went on. "So you could talk about that if you run out of other things to say."

"I'm outta here."

Charlie stood and nearly tripped over his chair. He shoved it under the table, crammed the last of the toast into his mouth, then scooped up a pile of books from the counter, fixing his sister with a deadly look.

"You know, Em, just when I think you couldn't get any dumber—"

"Charlie, she's always been crazy about you," Emma said calmly, joining him at the door. "And you're the dumb one if you haven't figured it out by now."

For the second time Charlie's mouth dropped open, though this time nothing came out.

Mrs. Donovan tried not to laugh. "Charlie, are you blushing?"

"He is blushing," Emma teased. "And not only that," she added, pulling him sideways to whisper in his ear, "you just let your guard down, Romeo."

Charlie's face was bright red. With as much dignity as he could muster, he shook Emma off and turned away, yanking his jacket from a hook on the wall.

"I love you two." Mrs. Donovan stood up and stretched. "Have a glorious day. And try not to kill each other."

Emma blew a kiss as their mother left the room. Charlie was still standing at the door but suddenly turned and leaned down over her.

"Tell you what," he said, lowering his voice to a near whisper. "I'll make you a deal."

"No deals." Emma frowned. She watched him a moment, then added suspiciously, "What kind of deal?"

Charlie looked immensely pleased with himself. "I'll ask Val to the dance if you spend one night in the Farmington house."

For a brief second Emma thought she'd misunderstood. She kept staring at him, waiting for him to say he'd only been joking.

"One night in the Farmington house," Charlie repeated. "Alone."

"Are you *crazy*? That's the most . . . the most . . . *no way!*"

"Too bad." Charlie clucked his tongue in reproach. "And you call yourself a best friend."

Anger bubbled inside her. She saw the triumph in Charlie's eyes, and that superior look he always got when he knew he'd won a battle.

Except he wasn't going to win this one.

She squared her shoulders and met his gaze. She heard herself speak, but her voice sounded very far away.

"When?" she challenged him.

A flicker of surprise crossed Charlie's face. She knew she'd shocked him, that he'd never really thought she'd agree to it.

"This Friday," he said. "Mom has a training seminar and won't be home."

"Fine. Friday it is."

He grinned at her and opened the door. "Oh, and remember—this is *our* little secret."

5

"This has been a horrible week." Val sighed, shoving books into her locker. "One of the worst weeks in my whole life."

Beside her, Emma balanced a stack of notebooks in the crook of one arm, mentally trying to review her homework for the weekend. "And why's that?" she asked absentmindedly.

"Oh, as if you didn't know!"

"I don't know. Enlighten me."

The two of them flattened back against the wall, waving at a surge of fellow students jostling past them. The last bell had rung for the day, and the noise was deafening—laughter, shouts, the slamming of doors. From what Emma could hear through the general chaos, everyone seemed to be talking about the winter dance. Banners draped from the ceilings, signs were posted everywhere on campus, and she and Val had spent most of the afternoon voting on last-minute decisions with the decorating committee.

The crowd began to thin. Val beamed a dazzling smile, called good-bye to one last straggler, then turned to Emma with a tragic expression.

"Everyone's been asking me who my date is, Em. What am I supposed to say?"

"I don't know," Emma hedged. "What *have* you been saying?"

"That I haven't made up my mind yet."

"Nice touch. Keep them guessing."

Val looked so forlorn that Emma quickly busied herself in her locker. Next to prom and graduation, Hartville High's winter dance was The Event of the year, and like so many others, Val had her heart set on going. Emma had already helped her pick out a dress; they'd already decided on the perfect hairstyle. And now that Val was dateless, Emma couldn't bear seeing her so disappointed.

Right. And how disappointed is she gonna be when she finds out about this bet with Charlie?

"Em, are you okay?"

Emma jumped. Guiltily she looked over at Val. "Why?"

"I don't know, you've just acted weird all week. You want to sleep over? Even though I'm grounded?"

"I can't." Emma thought fast. "I might have the flu."

As if in confirmation, her stomach cramped. Val could *never* know about tonight, Emma swore to herself. As determined as she was to win this dare, she was even more determined to keep it from her best friend.

If Val ever found out the truth, it would ruin everything.

Ignoring Val's puzzled frown, Emma slammed the door of her locker. "Come on," she said, taking Val's arm. "Charlie'll kill us if we don't hurry."

Together they made their way outdoors and to the parking lot. Charlie was waiting in his car, eyes closed and head tilted back, rock music blaring full-blast. He didn't even notice them till Emma jerked open the passenger door and snapped off the radio.

"One second," he greeted them lazily. "One more second and you were both walking."

Emma slid in beside him. "Take Val home."

"What am I, your private chauffeur?" He started the car before they were settled, then glanced at Val in the rearview mirror. "My, my, aren't we looking grumpy."

Val raised an eyebrow in warning. "Don't mess with me, Charlie. It's Friday, and I'm not even allowed to enjoy it." She made a sad, wistful sound in her throat. "I guess I'll just sit home alone and *pretend* I'm having fun."

"You *would* be out having fun, if you hadn't stolen your mom's Mercedes yesterday," Charlie reminded her.

Emma kept her attention focused out the window. She didn't dare look over at her brother—she knew she'd see that infuriating grin on his face. Her stomach knotted even more. How had she even managed to keep their little secret all week? It had gnawed at her relentlessly; all she'd been able to think about was the Farmington house and their stupid bet. She really *did* feel like she was coming down with the flu.

For the moment Val didn't seem to notice her silence. She was still too busy arguing with Charlie.

"I didn't steal it," Val said firmly. "I borrowed it because mine was in the shop."

"Right."

"Well, how was I supposed to know Mom was on call for the emergency room last night?" Val grumbled, smacking the back of Charlie's head. "Anyway, I've repented long enough."

Charlie pinched his lips together and did his best impression of an overbearing mother. "This is good for you, Valerie. This will teach you the meaning of responsibility."

Val smacked him harder. Wincing, Charlie laughed and pulled to the curb in front of Val's house.

"Emma? Are you sure you're okay?" Val leaned forward and touched her friend's shoulder. "You haven't said a word all the way home."

"Oh, she's just thinking about the weekend," Charlie replied casually.

"Really?" Val asked. "Is there something exciting going on that I don't know about?" Her lips slid into a pout. "That I'm not going to be part of?"

Emma shook her head. "No. Just my usual boring life."

She frowned at her brother, who widened his eyes in mock anticipation.

"But you just never know what *might* happen, right, Em?" he taunted.

"Charlie, what is *with* you?" Val rolled her eyes and shoved open the door. "I'll call you tomorrow, Em." And then, at Emma's vague nod, she added, "You *really* don't look too good. Are you sure you don't want some company tonight? You could bring over a pizza, and we could try that new lavender tint on your hair."

Emma tried to shut out the pleading in Val's tone. "I . . . I can't," she said lamely. "I . . . wouldn't want you to catch this bug, or whatever it is I have."

"Wow," Charlie declared solemnly, patting her other shoulder. "What a friend, Em. Really. You are *one, good, true* friend. I mean, really. The truest."

"Charlie, whatever it is you're up to," Val said, letting herself out of the car, "I'm sure Emma's on to you. You're about as subtle as a freight train."

The girls waved to each other till Charlie's car rounded the corner. Then Emma faced him with a scowl.

"You are such a jerk, Charlie. I think I've changed my mind. I don't think I want you having anything to do with Val."

Charlie burst out laughing. "I knew it! I *knew* it! I *knew* you wouldn't go through with it—I knew you'd make some excuse at the last minute!"

"Oh, you did? Well, here's a news flash for you," she retorted angrily. "I'm still gonna spend the night at the Farmington house, even though I *don't* want my best friend going out with you!"

For a brief second Charlie looked surprised. As Emma glared at him, he turned his eyes back to the road, and they finished the ride in silence.

Twilight was already falling when they pulled into the driveway. Mom had left a meatloaf to be heated, but Emma couldn't eat a bite. Instead she went up to her room and took another survey of her camping gear:

sleeping bag and extra blanket, flashlight, cell phone. A paperback romance, her headset, a jumbo bag of potato chips, three candy bars, and two diet Cokes. She didn't plan on doing much sleeping tonight. *If I can just keep busy till sunrise, then I won't have time to be nervous . . . .*

"Ready?"

With a start Emma swung around to see Charlie lounging in the doorway.

"Of course I'm ready," she grumbled. "Don't I look like I'm ready?"

"I'll help you take your stuff."

Emma started to tell him to go away, then changed her mind. *Not that I need him,* she assured herself, *but why should I do all the work?* As they went outside, she noticed that deep shadows had already thickened around the house, and the wind was picking up, whining through bare trees.

Silently they cut through the yard. When they finally reached the fence, Charlie boosted her over, tossed Emma her things, then climbed down after her. The Farmington house looked more forbidding than ever as the two of them made their way around to the front. Huge drifts of leaves nearly obscured the sagging porch, and a splintered porch swing hung lopsided from one rusty chain, scraping back and forth across the broken floorboards. With minimal effort Charlie pried open the carved wooden door, and as it groaned on its hinges, Emma fought down an overpowering urge to run.

"This is as far as I go," Charlie said. "You're on your own from here."

"Fine." Emma wouldn't give him the satisfaction of seeing how scared she was. Quickly she stalled for time.

"You could . . . you could at least make sure nobody's hiding in there."

"Okay." Charlie shrugged. He cupped his hands to his mouth and shouted, "Hey, is anybody hiding in there?"

"That's not funny, Charlie!"

The silence was as dark and heavy as the shadows pressing around them. After listening a minute more, Charlie grinned and shrugged again.

"Okay, satisfied?"

Before Emma could answer, a cold gust of wind whipped out at them across the threshold, slamming the door and shuddering the warped boards beneath their feet.

Both of them jumped back. As Charlie's arm slid protectively around her shoulders, Emma choked down her fear and wriggled away from him.

She fixed him with an accusing stare.

"What?" Charlie demanded. "I didn't do that, if that's what you're thinking."

Yet Emma could tell he was nervous now. He looked first toward one end of the porch and then the other. Finally he looked back at Emma.

"Okay, okay." He tried to laugh, but it came out sounding strained. "Joke's over."

Emma wasn't amused. "What do you mean, 'joke's over'?"

"I mean, it's fine." He cleared his throat, scanned the porch again, and shifted from one foot to the other. "I mean, I knew you wouldn't really stay; I just wanted to see how far you'd go. So come on."

"Come on where?" Emma held her ground.

"Home, and stop being so dense." Charlie reached out for her, but she straightened indignantly and stepped farther away. "Come on, Emma, you know you're terrified of this place—you've been agonizing over it all week!"

"So what you're saying is, you never actually thought I'd go through with it?"

"I was always *positive* you wouldn't go through with it. But you got this far, and that's farther than I thought you'd go. So come on home."

"You're out of your mind. If you're so scared about it, you can leave. But I'm not going anywhere."

Charlie heaved a sigh. "Cut it out, Em. I'm not the one who's scared, and we're going home. Mom'd kill me if she found out I left you here alone, and you know it."

"Just get away from me, Charlie." Emma's voice was tight with rage. She knew she was overreacting, but it was more than Charlie's teasing now, more than Val's date for the dance. It was a matter of saving face, and she wasn't about to back down, no matter how frightened she was. "I said I'd stay, and I'm staying! I don't back out on my promises!"

"It wasn't a promise! It was a *joke*!" Charlie lunged for her, but again she managed to dodge him. "Come on, Em—stop being such a brat!"

Ignoring him, Emma glanced quickly at the house. The front door had come open again while they were arguing, and now it creaked gently back and forth, back and forth, as though daring her to enter. She gulped and turned her attention back to Charlie.

"It's not like you lost the bet," Charlie was still trying to reason with her. "I mean, I'll still ask Val to the stupid dance if that's what you want."

"Oh, yeah, and hold this over my head for the rest of my life—"

"I won't! I swear! Will you just calm down and—"

"*I'm staying!*" Emma shouted at him. And then, as he rolled his eyes, she repeated, "I'm staying. And that's final."

Charlie opened his mouth, hesitated, then closed it again. "Okay. Fine. Great. You and all the spirits have a grand old time."

"I'm sure we will," Emma retorted.

"And if Mom finds out, I'm telling her this was all *your* idea. I'll say I thought you were in your room sleeping all night and didn't know anything about it."

"I don't care. Tell her whatever you want. She won't believe *you* anyway."

Charlie looked like he might make a grab for her again. Emma backed away.

"Em." That condescending tone was creeping into Charlie's voice now, that tone Emma hated so much. "Just come home with me. Don't be stupid."

Emma turned her back on him, walked to the front door, and put her hand on the doorknob. She heard Charlie's sound of exasperation as he stomped down the steps.

For a split second her heart leaped into her throat. The thought of calling Charlie back loomed in her mind, and she tried to force it down. She watched him stop. He froze midstride and turned slowly back to look at her.

"You got the phone, right?" he asked grudgingly

Emma gave him a thumbs-up. "Right."

"Well . . ." He looked flustered, as though he hadn't really planned on saying what he was about to say. "Well . . . call me . . . you know . . . if you need—"

"Don't hold your breath, Charlie."

She saw him glower at her, and then he disappeared into the darkness.

She waited till she heard him scale the fence and drop down on the other side, till she could no longer hear his fading footsteps through the dead leaves in their yard. Then she let go of the doorknob and backed very slowly to the edge of the porch.

Emma had absolutely no intention of stepping foot inside this creepy old house. With her sleeping bag and supplies, she figured she could spend the night just as easily outside as in, and no one would ever be the wiser.

Turning around, she peered anxiously over the tangled lawn. It'd be just like Charlie and his pals to sneak back later and try to scare her, so she'd have to camp in the perfect spot. Somewhere hidden and not too far from the house, so she could watch them all make total fools of themselves. She'd let Charlie suffer awhile when he couldn't find her. *Then I'll sneak up on the whole stupid bunch of them and give them the scare of their lives.*

Feeling immensely proud of herself, Emma aimed her flashlight and walked carefully back along the wraparound porch. The structure groaned beneath her weight, and there were gaping holes from dry rot and termites. She pressed close to the wall, holding her breath as she passed several long, narrow windows. Some of the panes were broken, the shredded lace of old curtains fluttering out like pale dead hands, and though she couldn't see through the shadows, she could feel the tiny hairs prickling at the back of her neck. Without warning she remembered the shadow she'd seen at the upstairs window, and that feeling—that *knowing*—of being watched. . . .

She'd been so certain someone was there that night.

And what if that someone's here now . . . just beyond the curtains . . . reaching out for me through the broken glass . . .

"Oh, God," Emma whispered.

She turned and ran, stumbling back along the porch, trying to reach the front steps.

She didn't hear the sudden snap of boards beneath her feet, the echo of her own scream as she plunged through cold, dank air. It only seemed in that one instant as though the whole world had collapsed around her in a choking cloud of dust and decay.

She fought to breathe but couldn't.

There was only the falling and the faraway panic, and then her mind went black.

6

❦

The first thing she saw was the rat.

It was crouched only inches from her hand, and as Emma gasped and lifted her head, the creature scurried off into the shadows.

I remember now . . . I fell. . . . I was running and I fell.

Pain jolted through her. As she tried to sit up, a dizzying flash of stars popped in her brain. Her whole body felt stiff and cold, and she could feel water seeping through her clothes. *Oh, God, where am I?*

Emma groped weakly, trying to find her flashlight. *Suppose the rat comes back. . . . Maybe the rats are everywhere, all around me and—*

Her mind broke off, confused. The flashlight was nowhere to be found, yet she realized now that she *could* see a little, that there was a pale sort of glow misting the air around her, bringing shadows and shapes into soft, hazy focus. Barrels . . . shelves full of dust-covered jars . . . crates and tools and baskets of apples . . .

A cellar? Moving cautiously this time, Emma squinted through the gloom. *I must have fallen through the porch and landed in the cellar.*

Before she could think anything else, there was a creaking sound from somewhere above her head, and a narrow beam of light slanted down across the floor at her feet. Terrified, she lay down again, but not before seeing a flight of wooden steps far off to her right, the open door at the top, and the tall figure of a man silhouetted there with a lantern.

"Emma!" a voice hissed. "Emma, are you down here?"

Emma's thoughts whirled in confusion. "Charlie?" she whispered, yet at the same time it didn't really sound like Charlie; it didn't really sound like anyone she recognized.

"Emma!" Once more the voice spoke, with urgency this time.

"I'm . . . I fell," she said stupidly and managed to prop herself on her elbows. *Of course it's Charlie, I'm just not thinking straight, who else would it be, no one even knows I'm here. . . .*

Immediately the figure began to descend. Emma could see the long legs, the dark pants, the lantern growing brighter. *Funny,* she thought distantly, *he doesn't walk like Charlie . . . he seems different somehow. . . .* Still dazed, she lifted one hand to shield her eyes from the light, and the figure stopped beside her.

"My God," he murmured, "what's he done to you this time?"

She moaned and took her hand away. He was kneeling beside her now, and she could see the mud on his boots, and she could smell horses and hay and wet leather, and *Charlie hates horses,* her mind kept spinning, and *Charlie doesn't have boots like that. . . .*

"No more," he said softly. "Do you hear me? *No more.* I'm going to get you out of here."

"What?" Emma whispered. She tried to see his face, but it was hidden in shadows; she tried again to place his voice—the deepness of it, the power of it, the kindness that suddenly made her want to cry.

Slowly he reached for her, and Emma stared down at his hand.

His touch was strong yet amazingly gentle. His fingers were long and slender, but even as they trailed down her cheek, she could feel their roughness, the scars of hard work.

Emma began to tremble. Instinct screamed at her to run, yet she felt oddly frozen in time, a captive of some strange dream. Her mind was foggy and faraway, yet she could hear this stranger calling her by name, she could feel him touching her face, and his touch was warm and all too real, and she couldn't move, she was rooted to the floor—

"Emma!"

She cried out as he gently took her shoulders.

"Please say something," he begged. "Don't you know me?"

He eased her into a sitting position and smoothed her hair from her eyes. His fingertips stroked down one side of her neck, and as he leaned even closer, Emma was able to see his face at last.

It took her breath away.

The sad intensity of his huge, dark eyes . . . his sensual lips . . . his long black hair, windblown about his face. She stared because she was terrified, because she was fascinated, because something in his gaze prevented her from looking anywhere else.

Another rat scurried along the wall, and as the young man glanced toward it, Emma quickly looked down. She could see his clothes now—the coarse material of his shirt; the long loose sleeves stained with mud and sweat; the way his shirt hung halfway open, revealing his chest. It was cold in here, every bit as cold as it had been outside, yet Emma could see a fine sheen of sweat glistening on his bare skin.

"Can you walk?" he asked.

She frowned slightly, trying to clear her head. *This isn't real—this can't be real. . . .*

"No matter," he said, not waiting for an answer. "I can carry you. Put your arm around my neck."

Emma lifted her eyes. A frightened sob rose into her throat, but she choked it down. "I can walk." She nodded. "I'm sure I can walk."

"Move your legs."

Emma did, and was surprised to hear a soft rustling sound. To her astonishment, she saw a tangle of long skirts and petticoats where her jeans should have been, and once more she froze, her head pounding. *I must be hallucinating—wake up, Emma, wake up!—you've got to wake up now!*

"Let me see if you've broken anything," he told her.

And then his hand was on her ankle, sliding slowly beneath her skirts, upward toward her thigh. She could feel the gentle pressure of his fingers as he searched for an injury, and she gasped aloud, only this time not in fear. Fire seemed to shoot through her veins, and she realized she was trembling all over. Quickly she put out her own hand and placed it over his, her heart nearly thudding out of control.

"I can get up," she insisted weakly. "Really. I'm perfectly all right."

"You're certain?"

Emma nodded. The stranger's arm went around her waist, and he lifted her as though she weighed nothing at all.

"Wait," Emma stopped him. Cautiously she leaned into him, and his hold on her tightened. "I don't understand this. I don't understand what's happening."

The young man's look was grave. "It's all right, Emma . . . you're only stunned from the fall. God, I wish you'd never have to remember the things he does to you. I *told* you one day he'd kill you, but you wouldn't believe me. Well, he's drunk himself into a stupor now . . . only this time you won't be here when he wakes up."

"Where are you taking me?"

"I won't stand by any longer and watch you suffering at his hands." The stranger stopped and turned her toward him. He peered earnestly into her face, and his voice grew husky with emotion. "I'm only sorry I didn't do something about it before now . . . even though you made me promise not to."

Emma stared, mesmerized, into the black depths of his eyes. His lips were only inches from her own. As they lowered and brushed lightly across hers, she shut her eyes and rested one hand upon his cheek.

She hadn't noticed the scar there before. His hair and the shadows must have hidden it, but now she could feel it—the long, jagged ridge that slashed across his left cheek.

"But you're the one who suffers. . . ." she said slowly, softly, and *why did I say that, how do I know that?* Her mind felt cloudy and confused, as though strange but familiar memories hovered just out of reach. "You're the one I'm afraid for."

"Don't be afraid for me, Emma. Just love me."

He clasped her to him with a passion Emma had never known. Her arms locked around his neck, and his lips blazed a fiery trail from her mouth, her cheeks, her eyelids, to the racing pulse at the base of her throat. She moaned softly and ran her fingers through the soft mane of his hair, tilting her head back as his kisses fell lower still, her torn dress sliding off one shoulder, his lips burning everywhere they touched.

She cried out and clutched him tighter. She heard herself whispering, over and over—she knew she was saying his name, yet at the same time her voice was eerily silent. Without warning he straightened, grabbed her elbows, and held her at arm's length.

"Not now," he said breathlessly. "There isn't time—"

"But you know I can't leave!" Emma glanced toward the door at the top of the stairs, a cold dread growing within her. Something bad lay beyond that door, she could sense it, something bad and evil and terrifying. As if from a great distance, she heard herself say, "He'll never let me go! He'll track me down until he finds me and then—"

"We'll leave together."

"And he'll kill us both."

The young man shook his head. "He'll never hurt you again. *Nothing* will ever hurt you again. I swear it, Emma. I swear it on my love for you."

She opened her mouth to speak, but he covered it with his own. She could feel the world spinning around her, reality falling far, far away, and for one magical instant, his love, his desperation, and his promise, reaching deep inside her, touching and taking her very soul.

Time stopped. Emma could hear the sound of her heart beating, and then both their hearts beating as one single entity. When he pulled away from her this time, she swayed slightly against him.

"You, of all people, know how dangerous . . . Father is," she murmured. *Yes . . . of course . . . it's all making sense . . . I'm remembering now. . . .* "What Father's capable of."

"Do you think that frightens me?" His mouth twisted into a derisive smile. "After seeing all he's done to you?"

"But it frightens *me*!" her voice rose, pleading. "I couldn't bear it if anything happened to you!"

Eyes flashing, he grabbed her by the shoulders. For a long moment he gazed at her, but then his tension began to ease, his hands sliding down her arms to her wrists.

"Nothing will happen to me," he said softly. "As long as I have you."

She started to answer, but he brushed her lips with a kiss. She watched as he took something from his pocket, as he slid it onto the third finger of her left hand.

It was a ring. A thin gold band with a tiny heart at its center.

"Oh, Daniel—" She spoke his name effortlessly, like breathing, but again he silenced her with a kiss.

When he finally drew back from her, Emma lifted one hand to his cheek. Emotions were coursing through her veins—emotions she couldn't control—yearning and sorrow and a horrible sense of foreboding. She leaned heavily against his chest. She felt his heartbeat, stronger now, and even more rapid than her own.

"Come," he said urgently. "We've got to hurry."

7

Daniel led Emma up the wooden steps.

Hand in hand they kept close to the wall, pausing at the very top to listen.

The door opened onto semidarkness. The house held its breath around them.

Emma watched as he blew out the lantern. Holding a warning finger to his lips, he guided her down a long, narrow hallway, and then through another door out onto a porch. Emma paused uncertainly, her eyes scanning the clean white floorboards, the painted porch swing, the cat curled up on its cushion. A vague thought struck her that she'd been here before, and very recently, but as soon as the thought began to take form, it was gone again, as quickly as it had come. She lifted her face to the moonlight. She could hear a dog barking in the distance, and wind sighing through trees, and once again she felt a curious detachment—as though she were both actress and audience in the same strange dream.

"You're shaking," Daniel said, almost apologetically. Emma realized he had his arm around her shoulders and that she was shivering from the cold. "We can't go back for dry clothes now—it's too dangerous."

She ran with him through the tall, dead grass, her long skirts wrapping around her legs, tripping her. Her slippers were so thin, she could feel the frost seeping through and numbing her toes. It took forever to reach the barn, and when they finally did she was gasping, her breath trailing in the air like soft pale clouds.

"Close the door," he ordered.

Emma did so. Pushing the barn door shut behind them, she watched while he relit the lantern and moved swiftly along the almost empty row of well-kept stalls, saddling up her own mare and her father's prize stallion. Even the horses seemed nervous tonight, starting at every shadow. Daniel spoke to them in low, gentle tones, running his hands smoothly over their necks and flanks until they calmed down.

"We might have an hour's headstart," he told Emma. "Two, if we're lucky. He'll never try to track us at night. We'll ride till daybreak and keep to the woods."

Emma felt a hollowness in the pit of her stomach. "You underestimate him. He won't stop until he finds me and brings me home. And . . ."

Her voice trailed away. He cast her a grim, knowing look.

"And sees me dead," he finished. "Well, that's not

going to happen. I know this countryside like the back of my hand—I know so many secret places, the devil himself couldn't find us. And once we cross the river—"

"It won't matter where we go," Emma reminded him softly. She stared into the lantern light, tears misting her eyes, as the cruel reality of their situation sank deep into her heart. *We're doomed if we leave . . . doomed if we stay.* She took a deep breath and added, "There won't be any place for us to hide. He'll have the whole county out looking for us."

Their eyes met and held. And as Emma stared into his face, such a surge of love and pain went through her that her heart seemed to burst into a million pieces.

"I love you, Daniel," she said.

She took a step toward him . . .

Then turned and screamed as the barn door crashed open behind her.

He was silhouetted there in the threshold—the man she hated most, feared most in the world. He was clothed in the color of his soul, self-righteous black from his hat to his shoes, with a Bible clutched in one hand and an empty bottle dangling from the other. His face was the face of a demon, twisted in a drunken rage, and before Emma could get away, he grabbed her savagely by the arm.

"No, Father!" she cried. "You're hurting me!"

But her father was past the point of hearing. He reeked of whiskey and vomit, and his grip was merciless.

"Where do you think you're going, Daughter?" he snarled. "Did you really think you could defy me and get away with it? Break God's commandments—'*Honor thy father!*'—and expect salvation? *Pride,* Daughter! Pride to think you could outsmart the Lord Almighty with your lustful, wicked ways and hope to avoid the fires of eternal damnation!"

"It's not what you think!" Emma pleaded. She tried to pull free, but his grip only tightened. "Please, Father, let's just go back in the house—"

"*Let her go!*" Daniel shouted. The horses whinnied, stamping nervously as he grabbed their reins and tried to control them. "Stand away from the door!"

A leering grin spread over her father's face. "And if I don't?" he taunted. "What might you do? Call upon Satan? Strike me dead?"

Daniel's voice was chilling. "If I have to."

"Please!" Emma was terrified now, more terrified than she'd ever been in her life. Her body felt strangely paralyzed, even as she finally managed to break free, even as she ran to the other side of the barn and threw herself into Daniel's arms. With one quick motion, he hoisted her into the saddle, then turned to mount his own horse.

"Go, Emma!" he commanded. "Go, and don't look back!"

Then everything happened too fast.

In the wildly flickering shadows Emma saw her father fall to his knees in the straw, then lunge forward again, hurling something through the air. She heard the cry of pain and surprise behind her, and as she looked around, she saw Daniel staggering backward, his eyes wide, his hands clutching at the pitchfork embedded in his chest.

"*No!*" she screamed. "*Daniel, no!*"

Emma's horse reared, throwing her. As she landed

hard against the barn wall, she instinctively covered her head to avoid the crashing hooves. Both horses were in a frenzy now, and she could hear her father's maniacal laughter.

"*Daniel!*" she screamed again.

She was trying to crawl, trying to reach him. As she lowered her arms, she saw one of the horses kick over the lantern, sending an instant explosion of flame into the air and across the floor. The two animals bolted, nearly trampling the old man, their shrieks of terror echoing with his wild ravings of damnation. In less than a heartbeat a fiery wall surrounded Emma, and as she stumbled to her feet, she saw her father follow the horses outside and shut the door behind him.

"*Help us!*" Emma shrieked. "*Oh, God, somebody help us!*"

Coughing and choking, she tried to find Daniel. Already the air was swirling with sparks and debris; the barn was a tinderbox, melting, collapsing around her. The smoke was so thick, she could hardly see, could hardly breathe. She dropped to her knees and again started to crawl.

"Daniel," she sobbed, "Daniel . . . no! Not now!— not like this!"

But Daniel didn't answer.

No one answered. And no one came to help.

Emma paused, gasping for breath. Her throat felt raw and swollen; her body was heavy, her head curiously light. She thought she heard her name being called. With a surge of hope, she followed the sound, dragging herself on her elbows. Blindly she groped her way into a stall and saw Daniel at last, sprawled on his back in a corner.

The pitchfork was gone. Somehow he'd managed to wrench it free, but Emma could see his shirt soaked with blood. The flames were closing in relentlessly now. She could smell the burnt fabric of her skirt, her scorched hair . . .

"I'm here, Daniel," she whispered. "Can you hear me, my love? I'm here . . . I'm here. . . ."

She knew she was losing consciousness. With one last effort she knelt beside him, cradling his head in her arms, desperately searching his eyes for some sign of recognition. His gaze was hazy and unfocused, yet slowly it fixed upon her face, and for one brief instant Emma thought he might have smiled.

"I'm here," she said again, but there was a deafening crash, a blistering surge of heat billowing over her in suffocating waves.

Emma pressed her face against Daniel's chest.

And then she turned her head, breathing deeply of the thick, black smoke, praying to die before she felt the flames.

8

"*Oh, God! Somebody please help us!*"

Emma screamed herself awake.

As her eyes snapped open, she felt a wave of nausea wash over her, and she swallowed hard, trying not to throw up. She was lying on her side, and she was freezing cold. Her whole body ached.

It was pitch dark where she was, but the faint beam of her flashlight still burned, aiming off into a corner toward a steep flight of wooden steps.

"*No!*"

Bolting upright, Emma gulped again as the darkness tilted around her. She felt a heaving sensation in her chest and suddenly realized she was crying.

"Please, somebody . . ." she mumbled again, but then her voice trailed off. She forced herself to take a calming breath. With shaking hands she pushed her hair back from her forehead and frowned.

She was covered with dirt. She could feel cobwebs tangled in her hair, and there was a sickening taste of dust and mildew in the back of her throat.

Where am I, anyway?

Must be some sort of cellar, she thought to herself, and for one split second it almost seemed familiar. She wondered why those steps in the corner seemed so fascinating. She couldn't stop staring at them, almost as if she expected a light to flicker down them at any moment.

A gleam of lantern light . . . two strong arms to hold me . . .

Emma's frown deepened. *What's that all about?*

She strained her ears through the darkness. She listened for the tread of footsteps, for the sound of a familiar voice.

But no one came.

There was only the silence and the racing of her heart.

Very slowly Emma crawled over and picked up the flashlight. For several minutes she played it over her surroundings, then aimed it steadily at the gaping hole above her head. She could see now that she'd fallen through the porch and landed on a damp pile of dirty blankets in the basement. *I could have been killed,* she thought suddenly, *and wouldn't that serve Charlie right, for Mom to come home and find me dead, and it'd be all his fault.*

In spite of herself she managed a laugh. Well, little more than a croak, really, but it did make her feel better. Her hand was still shaking; she could hardly hold on to the flashlight. Quickly she sat down again, cross-legged on the floor, trying to pull herself together.

What's wrong with me? I'm acting like an idiot!

She stared down at her dirty jeans. One knee was throbbing, and she could see a rip there, stained with dried blood. She felt like crying, like running away and never coming back here—yet at the same time she couldn't bring herself to do it, couldn't bring herself to leave this house.

She pressed both hands to her eyes. She took a deep, steadying breath, then rubbed gingerly at her forehead.

I'm having a condition, she told herself firmly, *some weird condition people get when they fall through porches.*

"Damn you, Charlie," she muttered out loud. "You'd better *marry* Val, for all I've gone through tonight!"

Painfully she got to her feet. It was obvious she couldn't get out the way she'd come in, so she headed cautiously for the stairs. There was an open doorway at the top, and as Emma stared at it, she had the eeriest feeling that she'd passed through it once before.

She stood a moment, thinking. Tiny bits of memory seemed to be hovering right at the edges of her mind, yet she couldn't quite call them into focus. She told herself she must have noticed the door as she'd fallen, or maybe she'd even roused once or twice from unconsciousness and seen it as she'd lain there on the floor. And yet, as she began to climb the steps, she knew somehow that there would be a long, narrow hallway on the other side of the threshold, and that it would lead her outside.

The hallway *was* there, exactly as she'd thought.

Emma shone her light over the walls and ceiling, cringing at the matted cobwebs, the dead bugs and spiders, the undisturbed layers of dust upon the floor. It had obviously been years since anyone had used this passageway, and yet there was a sense of urgency here—she could *feel* it!—something desperate and very frightened. It hit her so hard that she gasped and dropped the flashlight, flattening herself against the back wall.

And then she remembered.

The dream—the vision—*all* of it came back with a rush, with such painful clarity that Emma cried out and covered her face with her hands.

She stood like that until every last detail had played itself out in her mind, and then very slowly she slid down the wall and onto the floor.

She felt completely drained. For a long while she simply sat there without moving, then she forced herself to pick up the flashlight again. "Have you totally lost your mind?" she groaned softly. "It was a *dream*! Just a stupid *dream*!"

She didn't want to remember anymore—didn't want to *think* anymore. Scrambling to her feet, she tried the door and was puzzled when it wouldn't open. In the dream it *had* opened—she recalled it clearly—in the dream it had opened to the front of the house; it had been an escape. *And Charlie opened it, too, without any trouble. . . . What's going on?*

For now, no matter how hard she pushed, it simply refused to budge. *Almost as if it doesn't want me to leave. . . .*

Nervously Emma spun around and shone the light toward the other end of the passageway. To her surprise she saw the outline of a second door, one that had been completely hidden there in the darkness. She could feel her panic mounting. This house was really getting to her, and she desperately needed some air. Taking a deep breath, she threw herself against the door and landed without warning into the room beyond.

It had probably been a fine kitchen once, but now it was sadly deteriorated, with warped, stained floorboards, huge gaps of peeling paint, and a stale chill in its walls. Emma shuddered and pulled her jacket tighter. Mice and rats had comfortably settled in, by the look of things. Several odds and ends of furniture—obviously antiques—had been shoved recklessly into corners, and an old-fashioned cookstove crouched near a boarded-up window. There was a fireplace covered in soot, a large table in the center of the room, and cast-iron pots and rusty utensils hanging from rafters in the ceiling, all of them strung with spiderwebs.

Like a museum, she thought, picking her way carefully across the floor. She slipped through another doorway and into an adjoining room. *A museum and a mausoleum.*

She didn't stop, and she didn't explore. She had the fleeting impression of dark, heavy furniture, shapeless objects draped in sheets, an oppressive atmosphere that had nothing to do with the musty air. She realized she was running now, looking frantically for a way out, going through a maze of rooms and hallways that seemed to lead absolutely nowhere. Her head was pounding; her heart felt ready to burst. When she finally spotted an outside door, she nearly wrenched it off its hinges trying to tug it open.

The door gave without warning.

Emma stumbled out into the night, only to find herself on the porch again, near the front of the house.

But she wasn't alone.

Before she could take another step, a tall figure detached itself from the darkness and reached out for her, cutting off her escape.

Emma screamed and bolted over the railing into the yard. The figure closed in—nearer and nearer—looming over her now—blotting out everything but her fear. She screamed again, and another cry drowned out her own.

"Jeez, Emma!" Charlie yelled. "You scared me to death!"

Emma froze. She thrust out her flashlight and immediately saw Charlie's pale face, Charlie's wide eyes staring back at her.

"I scared you!" Emma echoed furiously. "*I* scared *you?*" She swung at him, but he caught her arm, nearly toppling her off balance.

"Calm down!" he shouted. "Stop yelling!"

"Calm down?" Emma's voice went even louder. "I don't *want* to calm down! I'm lucky I'm even *alive!* I hate you, Charlie, I'll never forgive you for this, I—"

"I know, Em, I know! *I'm sorry!*"

At this unexpected apology, Emma went still. Slowly she ran her flashlight beam down the length of Charlie's body, her anger fading to total dismay. Charlie wasn't wearing shoes or a jacket. He stood there shivering in his socks and jeans and T-shirt, as though he'd run out of the house in a great hurry. But more than that, he looked frightened.

Really frightened.

For a long moment Emma just stared at him. And then she asked, "What are you doing here?"

Charlie seemed at a complete loss for words. After opening and closing his mouth several times, he finally shrugged and made a vague gesture with one arm.

"I fell asleep," he said quietly. "After I left you, I went home and was watching TV, and I fell asleep. And I had this dream. . . ."

Emma could feel her own face going pale now. "What . . . what was it about?"

"I'm not sure." He shook his head and clenched his jaw tightly. "But *you* were in it. Or maybe not you, but a girl who *looked* like you. And some other people I couldn't really see, just shadows. But it was like I could watch what was going on, at a really far distance—you and somebody trying to get away, and then this old man came in, and there was a fight. I could feel all this fear and confusion, all this panic, and then the fire started. I knew everyone was gonna die—and *they* knew they were gonna die. It was horrible, and it was so *real* . . . and when I woke up, I . . ."

Emma put a hand on his arm, but Charlie didn't notice. He shook his head again, sounding miserable.

"I really thought there *was* a fire, that you were trapped over here and couldn't get out. It was all mixed up—I *knew* I was awake by then, but it seemed like the dream was still going on. I mean, I could *hear* it—I could hear the screams, the roof collapsing. I could even smell the smoke. And I just started running. I just ran out of the house and came over, only there wasn't *anything*. No fire. Nothing."

Emma nodded slowly. She took a deep breath and started to tell him about her own experience, but before she could speak, Charlie frowned and took hold of her wrist.

"You're bleeding," he said.

"I know. I scraped my knee when I—"

"No, not your knee."

Puzzled, Emma looked down at the trickle of blood running over the back of her hand. The blood was coming from one of her fingers, where something had cut deeply into her skin.

"It's this," Charlie told her. "You must've scraped it on something."

Emma's heart froze in her chest. As she gazed down at the third finger of her left hand, she felt an anguished cry lodge helplessly in her throat.

She was wearing a ring.

A thin gold band with a tiny heart at its center.

9

"Where'd this come from?" Emma demanded. Her voice rose, thin and trembling, not her own voice at all. "This can't be . . . I mean . . . where'd this *come* from, Charlie?"

Charlie looked at her in total bewilderment. "What are you asking me for?"

"No, you don't understand! This can't *be* here, it's impossible!"

Charlie just stared at her. At last he said hoarsely, "Emma, what's going on?"

But Emma couldn't answer.

All she could do was stare at the ring on her hand as the night spun black around her, as the memory of the dream came back again, echo by echo, scene by vivid scene.

At last she reached out and carefully slipped the

ring off. She was shaking so badly, she almost dropped it. She could feel Charlie's curious gaze upon her as she turned the ring over and over, as she delicately traced the outline of the tiny heart with her fingertip. Her knees began to buckle, and she sat down hard upon the ground.

Charlie sat beside her. Still shivering, he rested his arms on his knees and fixed her with another stare.

"I never should have made that bet with you," he said softly. "It was stupid. I'm sorry."

Emma shook her head at him. This whole thing was too bizarre, too incredible. For one crazy second she actually wanted to believe that somehow, some-time, maybe Charlie had managed to slip the ring onto her finger when she wasn't looking. That this was all just part of some cruel joke Charlie had been planning for days.

Except she knew better.

She knew Charlie better than anyone did—and she could tell he wasn't faking. She kept her eyes on him now, and her voice came out wearily.

"I'd decided to sleep outside and just tell you I'd been in the house. But then I fell through the porch, and I must have blacked out for a while. . . ." She closed her eyes, not wanting to remember any more, but needing to get it all out. "Something happened tonight, Charlie. Something I can't explain . . . something . . . I don't know, maybe not of this world. And I was part of it."

Charlie's look grew more intense. "What do you mean?"

"I mean, I think you and I had the same experience. Whatever it was."

"I'm still not following."

"When I woke up in the cellar, someone came and rescued me."

"Who? You mean someone *has* been staying in the house, and we didn't know?"

"No. No, that's not it." Emma spoke slowly, her brow furrowed in thought. "Look, I know this is gonna sound crazy, but it was someone who knew me—or knew the person I was in the dream. He called me Emma. He was . . . well . . . we were . . . in love with each other."

She waited for Charlie to laugh, but he didn't. He just watched her, eyebrows raised, lips slightly parted.

Emma started again. "It all seemed so natural, like I'd just stepped into a play where I knew all the lines. He got me out of the house, and we made it to the barn, but my father—I mean, the other Emma's father—came in, and there was a terrible fight, and Daniel—the guy who rescued me—got—"

She broke off. Without warning, Daniel's eyes filled her mind, gazing at her with the sorrow of impending death. Emma could feel her own eyes filling with tears, and though she forced the image away, her voice was quivering.

"I can't even tell you how horrible it was. Seeing him die . . . and then the fire starting, and—"

"And you were trapped," Charlie finished quietly.

His sister nodded.

"So that's the part I saw," Charlie confirmed. He rubbed distractedly at the goose bumps on his arms. "Fire shooting up everywhere, and people fighting but no faces. Just shadows where their faces should have been. *Everyone* was shadows except for you."

He was silent a long time. Emma could see the careful control of emotions over his face, but it was obvious the dream had affected him deeply—much more deeply than he wanted to admit.

"Charlie, this wasn't just a dream," she said at last. "I can't explain it, but it's like the feeling *you* woke up with—you were so *sure* I was trapped over here in a fire. And I was convinced this whole experience really happened. Like the reality of the dream carried over into the reality of being awake."

"But you were still inside when you woke up?"

"Yes, in the cellar. In fact, I just kept lying there for a while, waiting for Daniel to come back down the steps and rescue me again. That's how real he was to me."

Charlie rubbed at his forehead. "Well, was he . . . you know, transparent or something?"

"If you mean was he a ghost, the answer's no. Or at least, he didn't *look* like a ghost. He was as solid as you and me. I touched him. He held me. He was warm and breathing and alive."

"But not really." Charlie seemed determined to make this point clear. "You hear what I'm saying, Em? In your mind, maybe, but not really alive, right?"

Emma made a sound of frustration. "I told you I can't explain it. I know what you're trying to say, but yes—at the time, in the experience—he *was* real."

"You could have been hallucinating. You know, from when you fell."

"But I wasn't. I remember trying to find my flashlight. I remember how my head was pounding. I *didn't* imagine that. And anyway, how else can you explain this?"

Emma looked down at the ring. Charlie said nothing.

"Daniel gave me this ring right before we went to the barn," Emma went on.

"You mean, he gave the other Emma a ring," Charlie corrected. "In the dream."

Emma ignored him. "Daniel gave me this ring, Charlie. I've never even *seen* this ring before tonight. If you're so sure this whole thing was some figment of our imaginations, then how'd this ring get on my hand?"

"Maybe you just don't remember. Maybe you had temporary amnesia or something and found it in the cellar and put it on. I mean, I've heard of that—temporary amnesia. From trauma and stuff."

Emma gave him a look.

"Okay," Charlie conceded. "Maybe not amnesia."

"Why are you arguing with me about this, Charlie?"

"I'm not—"

"Yes, you are." Angrily Emma jumped up. "You always act weird like this when you're scared."

"Scared? I'm not the one who just came screaming out of the house," he said irritably, getting to his feet. "I'm tired, and I'm freezing my butt off. And I'm just trying to figure stuff out."

"Well, so am I. And I'm still wondering why you and I would've experienced this thing at the same time."

Charlie glowered at her. He clamped his arms around his chest and huddled into himself for warmth. After a moment of mulling things over, he began reasoning out loud. "Okay. You said you blacked out—I could have been picking up your thoughts while you were unconscious. We were both in a sleep state, no barriers to keep anything out."

"But you don't usually see a lot of details in my dreams," Emma reminded him. "You pick up more on sensations and feelings, and maybe a scene or two. Only this time it was like you saw a whole movie, and you thought it was *real*. And the weird thing is, I felt like I was *in* this movie, but *watching* this movie at the same time."

"I know," Charlie admitted reluctantly. "That's sorta how I felt when I woke up and ran over here. Like I was still in my dream, but *not* in my dream."

"It doesn't make sense. Are you sure you didn't recognize any of those people?"

"No. Just you."

"Then it couldn't *really* have been me, could it? Trapped in some *Wizard of Oz* thing? I've never seen any of those people before, either!" She hesitated, then added, "Well, not in this life, anyway."

Charlie gave a snort of laughter. "So what are you saying? Reincarnation? Time travel?"

"I don't know what I'm saying," Emma returned impatiently. "But this ring . . ." She held it close to the flashlight. "How could a ring have crossed over from one . . . *what*?—dimension?—into another one?"

Charlie didn't answer. Instead he took the ring and slid it easily back onto the third finger of her left hand. It was a perfect fit.

Emma stared down at it. A painful chill cut straight through her heart.

"I think this is what happened," Charlie said slowly, still rationalizing aloud. "You fell into the cellar. You started looking for your flashlight. The ring was lying there on the floor. And you didn't even think about it, you just picked it up and put it on."

"Even from you, that's lame, Charlie. Don't you think I'd remember doing all that?"

"Okay." Charlie didn't bat an eye. "How about this, then? Maybe you picked up some weird vibes from the house—accidentally connected with some bad house-memories. Like, if the house is haunted, then maybe it used you as a sort of transmitter."

Emma considered the theory, though she said nothing. Charlie reached over, took the ring back from her, and put it in one pocket of his jeans.

"Or here's the best yet. Are you listening to me?" He enunciated each word slowly. "You had a night-mare, Em. Just leave it at that."

For a long moment the twins simply stared at each other. And then without warning, Emma began to cry.

Charlie wasn't prepared for tears. After an uncomfortable pause, he sighed and slipped his arms awkwardly around her.

"I loved him, Charlie," Emma sobbed. "Whoever he was—whoever *I* was—I loved him *so much,* and it's like I can still feel that part of it. Here, deep inside. And when I saw him die . . ."

Charlie's nod was almost imperceptible. "It broke your heart," he whispered. "I know. I felt it."

"So how'd I get caught up in all this?"

She heard him sigh again. She could feel him gently chafing her arms, trying to warm her up.

"Come on, Em," he finally said. "It was just a *dream*. You had a nightmare, and I happened to tune into it, and that's all it is. You're making way too much out of this—"

"How can you say that? You can't even explain how some strange ring ended up on my finger—"

"Maybe it was lodged in the porch all these years. Maybe when you fell through the boards, it came loose and got on your finger—"

"Oh, Charlie, come on!"

"Okay, I don't know how it got there. I don't." Releasing her, Charlie stepped back and made a gesture of surrender. "I wanna believe it's explainable. I wanna believe it's just some sort of weird coincidence, that it doesn't have anything to do with anything."

Her brother looked so frustrated that Emma had to smile. "You're just trying to make me feel better."

"Well . . . yeah. Mostly."

"But can't we find out?" Sniffling, she wiped the back of her hand across her nose. "We've got to find out something about the house, just so we'll be sure."

"Why would you even want to? Look how upset you are—why make it any worse?"

"Because I have to know. I need to understand."

Charlie's eyes narrowed. He bent his head, and she could hear him muttering to himself. "I'm being punished. I'm being punished for making this stupid bet. What was I thinking? I've created a monster. . . . What was I thinking of. . . ."

"Are you gonna help me or not?" Emma demanded. "There must be something in this town about the history of the Farmingtons and their house. Old newspaper records or—"

"Fine, I'll help you. Can we just go? I can't even feel my legs anymore."

Sheepishly Emma realized how cold he must be.

She pulled off her jacket, and he gratefully put it on.

"Where's your stuff?" he asked.

"In the cellar. And there's no way I'm going back for it now."

"For once, you're making sense. We'll do it tomorrow. In the nice, safe daylight."

Together they walked back to their house, relieved to set foot in the bright, warm kitchen. A sweatshirt lay wadded on the tabletop along with dirty dishes, a carton of milk, and empty soda cans; Mom's Friday night meatloaf sat cold and uneaten in a pan on the counter. Rolling her eyes at Charlie's mess, Emma went straight to the cupboard to make hot chocolate.

"You really banged yourself up," Charlie noticed, pointing to the rips in her jeans. "You'd better put something on those cuts."

Emma nodded glumly. Somehow bruises and scraped knees seemed unimportant in the general scheme of events. She sliced off a chunk of meat and nibbled at the edges, not really tasting it.

"So where do we start?" she asked.

Charlie threw her jacket over the back of a chair. He pulled his sweatshirt off the table and gave it a shake, sending a shower of crumbs across the floor.

"I don't know." His voice was muffled as he slid the sweatshirt over his head. "Library, maybe? City hall?"

"Is there anyone still living around here who might know something about the house?"

"You mean somebody really old? Like the crazy Miss Lobergs?"

"Forget it. I'm not asking them anything," Emma

insisted, ignoring Charlie's grin. She'd often seen the sisters taking an evening stroll in front of the house, and sometimes browsing together at the library on weekends, but she'd never had the courage to actually speak to them. Now she added, "This seemed like it happened a pretty long time ago, Charlie. Even *they* might not be *that* old."

"Maybe there's a historical society or something."

"I've never heard of one. Not in Hartville."

"Newspapers, then. There's bound to be something on the Internet."

Halfheartedly, Emma nodded. She swallowed her last bite of meatloaf and fixed Charlie with a solemn stare. "We can't tell anyone about this, you know."

"Hey, no problem. You think I'm gonna have everyone thinking you're some kind of mental case? Or that *I* am?"

In spite of herself, Emma smiled. She folded her arms across her chest, watched him a moment longer, then added slyly, "And what about Val?"

Charlie stared back at her. "What *about* Val?"

"Charlie Donovan, I went through *all this* because of that stupid bet, and you're gonna stand there and tell me—"

"I'll ask her! I'll ask her!" Charlie held up his hands and backed away in mock fear.

"When?" Emma demanded. She could practically see the wheels spinning in his head. If there was any possible way out of his agreement, she knew he'd try to find it. "Tell me when, Charlie—"

"Don't worry! I'll *do* it!"

"You'd better do it."

"I said I would."

"Then do it now. I want to actually *hear* you ask her on the phone."

Without missing a beat, Charlie gestured toward the kitchen clock. "Right, Em—it's one o'clock in the morning!"

"Is it?" Surprised, Emma glanced up at the clock, then back at her brother. She could see the triumph in Charlie's eyes, and for a second she felt strangely disoriented. "That's funny . . . I feel like . . ." She put a hand to her temple and frowned. "I feel like it should be later. I feel like I've been gone for . . ."

"Years?" Charlie snickered.

The mood changed abruptly. As Emma frowned at him, Charlie went quiet. He reached into his pocket, pulled out the ring, and carefully placed it on the table. For several minutes the two of them simply stood there and stared at it. It was Charlie who finally broke the silence.

"You should take that back to the house tomorrow. And leave it there."

"No." Emma shook her head. "You take it. I don't even want to look at it again."

Not giving him a chance to answer, she left the kitchen and went upstairs.

She sat in the dark for a long, long time, unable to sleep. All she could do was peer from her window out into the darkness, over at the house next door.

She tried to shut her mind to the memories. To convince herself that Charlie was right, that what had happened to her tonight was nothing more than a bad fall, a bad headache, a bad dream. As every scene played back to her in slow motion, she covered her face with her hands and tried desperately to resist the emotions that accompanied them, but the dream face . . . *Daniel's face* . . . refused to go away.

Emma rubbed a hand across her eyes, smelling the sweet, lingering scent of bathpowder. The shower she'd taken had washed away all the dirt and blood, but not the sensation of Daniel's hands caressing her body. She could still feel his touch upon her bare skin . . . the heat of his lips against her throat. . . . A slow warmth spread through her, yet Emma shivered and pulled her robe tight around her.

A ghost, Charlie had suggested. *Daniel . . . a ghost.*

She'd never believed in ghosts before . . . never thought much about them at all.

And she'd certainly never expected to fall in love with one.

10

"So what did you do?" Val demanded. She pushed her way in as Emma opened the back door, and she looked very, very suspicious.

"Hello to you, too." Emma yawned. "What time is it?"

Val used her no-nonsense tone. "You know I'm never out of bed before noon on weekends. So did you pay him, or sell your soul to the devil, or what?"

"What are talking about?" Emma was trying hard to focus. She hadn't fallen asleep till almost six this morning, hadn't roused again until Val's insistent knocking. Her eyes were swollen and blurry, and her brain felt like cotton. She shook her head and started back into the kitchen, leaving Val to shut the door.

"Hey." Val was looking more suspicious than ever. "Are you okay? You look like hell."

This time Emma managed a nod. "Yeah. That about describes it, all right."

"So what's up? I've been banging on that door for nearly ten minutes. Where's your mom?"

"Working an extra shift. Why?"

"'Cause something's extremely weird around here this morning."

"It's always weird around here. What makes this morning any different?"

"Come on!" Val wailed. "Stop acting like you don't know what I'm talking about!"

"But I really don't—" Abruptly Emma broke off. As she stared at her best friend, a jumble of memories began sorting themselves into her foggy brain. *The Farmington house . . . last night . . . the bet with . . . Charlie.* She closed her eyes, pressed one hand to her forehead, and tried again. "I really don't know what you're talking about."

This time Val didn't look quite so suspicious. She looked confused. "Honest?"

"Val, come on, I'm too tired for twenty questions." Emma yawned again and poured a cup of coffee. Val grabbed a handful of cookies from the jar on the counter and sat down at the table, watching her.

"Charlie called me this morning," she announced.

Emma raised an eyebrow. Her cup paused halfway to her lips. "Called you what?"

"I'm serious. Charlie called me this morning and asked me to the dance."

It was easy to look shocked, Emma realized. She already felt so dazed from last night, she was sure she came off as genuine.

"Charlie called you? For a *date*?"

"I know, I couldn't believe it, either." Val leaned across the table and put her hand on Emma's. Her voice lowered. "What do you think he's up to?"

Emma studied her friend closely. On the outside, Val was making an extraordinary effort to appear nonchalant, but her eyes were glowing with excitement. Emma swallowed a sick taste of guilt and reminded herself that her intentions were noble.

"I have no idea." Emma squeezed Val's hand. "Maybe—for once—he's not up to anything. Wow, Val, that's . . . that's really . . . How do you feel about it?"

"Well, you know. I mean, I wouldn't want to hurt his feelings or anything by turning him down."

"Of course not," Emma was quick to agree. She could see Val eyeing the kitchen doorway, and she turned a little in her chair.

"Is he here?" Val whispered.

"I don't know. I just woke up. *Charlie!*" Emma directed her shout toward the hall, but got no answer.

Val pinched her arm. "Shh! No, don't call him!"

"Why not? I thought you wanted to see—"

"No, I don't want to see him. I just want to know what's going on. If he's temporarily lost his mind, or if he's made a bet with his stupid friends, or if I'm going to end up being some big joke."

Emma took a long sip of coffee. "Well, how'd he ask you, exactly? Are you sure it was Charlie?"

"I'm sure; I'd recognize that voice anywhere. First he insulted me like he always does, and then he said he didn't have a date for the dance and would I like to go."

"Sounds . . . romantic."

Val peered earnestly into Emma's face. "You mean you really didn't know? I can't believe you really didn't know."

"Val, you know Charlie never tells me anything personal." Emma looked totally serious. "And he *especially* wouldn't tell me if it involved you."

"Well, he might have been thinking it. Was he thinking it?"

"Oh, for heaven's sake—I can't see every single thought Charlie's thinking. Thank God."

Val settled back in her chair and frowned. "I just don't get it. I mean out of the clear blue, he just calls and asks me out?"

"Well, remember what I said about Roger? About how a lot of the guys were probably just waiting for him to be out of the picture?"

"Charlie's known me for almost four years. Long before Roger." Val munched awhile on her cookie. Then she groaned. "Oh, God, you don't think he feels sorry for me, do you? I couldn't stand it if he just asked me out of pity."

"He's not that sensitive," Emma reminded her. "Or that perceptive. He's a guy."

"Right. But *you're* sensitive and perceptive. Are you sure *you* weren't feeling sorry for me? Please tell me you didn't blackmail him or something awful like that."

Emma nearly choked on her coffee. Grabbing a napkin, she pressed it quickly to her mouth. "Hot," she mumbled. "Ouch, that's hot! And really, Val, I can't believe you're even saying that. If I was gonna pay someone to take you out, don't you think I'd have higher standards than to pick *Charlie*? For my best friend!"

Val seemed properly chastised. "You're right. I'm sorry."

"I mean, why would I pick Charlie—he's such a pain, not to mention he's like a brother to you. You guys fight almost as much as he and I do!"

Val's expression struggled between hope and disappointment. As Emma watched, a fresh surge of guilt swept through her, and she fidgeted miserably in her chair.

Finally Val nodded. "You're absolutely right. And I'm sure this isn't really a date. Not a *date* date, anyway. He probably just wants someone to hang out with."

"Val, if that's all he wants, he could have asked *me* to the dance."

Val paused again, mulling this over. "Then there might be some ulterior motive after all. He could be using me."

"For what?"

"I don't know. To make his girlfriend jealous?"

"Charlie doesn't have a girlfriend."

"Oh, come on, Emma, Charlie has a million girlfriends. Every girl in school, from freshmen on up."

"But not just *one* special *one,* is what I meant. At least not that I know of."

"But that's just the point. You just said he never tells you anything personal—he might have a girlfriend you don't know anything about. In fact, maybe he's been in love with some girl for a really long time, and you've never even suspected."

Emma stared at her friend, suddenly remembering back to the other morning. *Mom and I were teasing Charlie about Val, and he got so flustered . . . and then for just a second he let his guard down. . . .*

"What's wrong?" Val asked suddenly. "Are you smiling or is that a look of pain?"

"What? Oh, it's nothing." Under normal circumstances Emma would have examined this line of thought in more detail, but right now she wasn't in the mood. In fact, her brain was feeling thicker than ever, and she was beginning to wish Val would leave. Tactfully she said, "Val, you know Charlie never does anything he doesn't really want to do. But if you don't want to go out with him, don't go. It's not like you have to—"

"No, no," Val said quickly. *A little* too *quickly*, Emma thought. "No, I told him I would. Out of curiosity, mostly. And, you know . . . to be polite."

Emma played along. "Of course."

"And don't tease him," Val added seriously. "If you tease him about it, then he'll be self-conscious, and if he's self-conscious, then he'll want to back out, and if he stands me up, everyone will find out and laugh at me, and then I'll have to kill myself."

"Okay, I swear," Emma promised. "But only 'cause I don't want your suicide on my conscience."

Val bounced in her chair. She looked relieved and immensely happy. "Okay, great. Now that I have a date, I need to go shopping for shoes to match my dress. You're coming, right?"

For a second, Emma looked blank. "Ummm . . . I can't today."

"How come?"

"I . . . uh . . . have to go to the library."

Val lifted an incredulous eyebrow. "You *do* realize this is Saturday? Has some strange sickness infected the whole family?"

"It's just that I have this . . . this research project coming up," Emma babbled. "I need to get some information on it by Monday, and I have to read a lot of books. And I have to turn in a major outline."

To her relief, Val didn't ask what class it was for. She only said again, "But this is *Saturday*."

"I know, but . . . I've put it off as long as I can, and the outline's got to be even more detailed than I thought. If I don't get it done today, I'll be in a panic."

"As usual," Val joked. "And as usual, you'll get an A, just like all the other assignments you panic over." Laughing, she got up and started for the door. "Okay, if you prefer books to bargain-hunting . . . Will you be home later?"

"Sure."

"Great. I'll call you. Maybe we can get together then, if you feel better."

"Yeah, maybe." Emma walked her to the door, and as the two of them stood there talking, Charlie suddenly burst in. His glance flicked briefly from one to the other, then he shouldered past them, pulling off his jacket as he went.

"Hey, Val," he mumbled. He didn't even look at Emma. Instead he disappeared into the hallway, and they heard him climbing the stairs, two at a time.

"Hey," Val answered, but the only response she got was the slam of Charlie's bedroom door. She and Emma stared at each other. Emma rolled her eyes.

"What was that?" Val demanded. "He didn't insult me. He didn't make fun of me. He didn't try and mess up my hair, or ask me about the cheerleaders with the big breasts who sit behind me in math class."

"He's in a mood," Emma concluded. "Mood *du jour*."

"Well, I hope he's not going to ignore me like this

at the dance," Val said irritably. "I can have better con-
versations with myself."

"And more intelligent ones, I'm sure."

Val stepped outside, then paused and turned back
to Emma. She put her hand on Emma's cheek.

"Em, are you sure you're okay?"

"Yeah, I'm fine," Emma assured her.

"I don't know . . . you still look really pale." Val
frowned, tilting her head to the side. "You just don't
seem like yourself this morning."

Emma forced a laugh. "Maybe I'm not." And then,
at Val's strange look, she added, "Oh, it's just your
imagination. You're just in shock over Charlie."

"I guess." Val regarded her another long moment,
then reached out for a hug. "You'd tell me if something
was bothering you, right?"

Another stab of guilt. "I just didn't sleep very well
last night," Emma said lamely.

Val pulled away from her and wrinkled up her
nose. "Well, no wonder. With that smell."

"What smell? What are you talking about?"

"That funny smell in your hair."

Bewildered, Emma ran one hand back over her
head. "My hair doesn't smell. I washed it last night.
With that new coconut cream shampoo you and I were
gonna try."

"Well, I'm glad *you* were the guinea pig." Val
laughed as she headed down the driveway to her car.
"That doesn't smell a bit like coconut. It smells more
like smoke!"

11

ᒥᒧᓇᒧᒥ

Emma shut the door and leaned against it.

Her stomach felt queasy, and she squeezed her eyes tightly shut, willing the nausea away.

It was just a joke; Val didn't mean anything by it. What she said was just a coincidence. . . .

Yet somehow Emma knew better. With an effort she pulled herself together and hurried upstairs to Charlie's room.

The music inside was deafening. Ignoring the RESTRICTED AREA: KEEP OUT sign on his closed door, Emma pounded and yelled Charlie's name. When the noise only got louder, she barged in uninvited and promptly tripped over a guitar lying just inside the doorway.

Emma squinted through the gloom and wrinkled

her nose in disgust. She hated coming in here; it was like the worst sort of obstacle course. Ever since Charlie'd decided to paint his walls black, the room had a murky feel to it even on the sunniest of days. Clothes were strewn everywhere—most of them dirty, she suspected, even though she and Charlie were each responsible for doing their own laundry. Ragged posters hung at various angles—rock groups, basketball stars, racing cars, bikini-clad models—and the ceiling was decorated with . . . well, no one was really sure what those weird splotches of colors were that Charlie painted on the ceiling when he was feeling out of sorts.

Emma's glance took in the desk littered with food wrappers, the Styrofoam cups spilling from the trashcan, and Charlie's prize collection of CDs overflowing the shelves on his wall, before she finally located her brother. He was practically invisible, sprawled flat across his unmade bed with his headphones on, and he glared at her as she yanked them off.

"Excuse me, but aren't you in the wrong room?" he asked coolly, wrestling the headphones away.

Before he could put them back on, Emma grabbed them again. "This is important, Charlie! Smell my hair!"

He looked at her like she was insane. "Kiss my butt!"

"I'm serious! Val said I smell like smoke! And after what happened last night . . . you know, the dream . . . the fire . . ."

Before he could protest, Emma leaned down in his face. Charlie batted her hair away and sat straight up.

"Well?" she demanded.

"I don't know," he said crossly. "Maybe just a little."

"Where'd you put the ring?"

"I thought you never wanted to see it again."

"I changed my mind." Determinedly, she switched on his bedside lamp. "Where'd you put it?"

Charlie jerked his chin in the direction of his desk. "Over there."

At once Emma went over and began pulling out drawers, rummaging through them with a vengeance. Charlie let out a yelp and practically leaped across the room.

"What do you think you're doing? Get outta there!"

"Well, where is it? Just tell me where it is and—"

"*I'll* get it!"

Charlie grabbed for her, but Emma stubbornly held on to the handle of the bottom drawer. As Charlie pulled her backward, the drawer suddenly popped out, spraying its contents all over the floor.

Surprised, Emma stared down at the mess. Charlie groaned and immediately dropped to his knees, trying to shovel everything back into a pile.

"Great. Nice work, Em. Really."

Emma ignored his sarcasm. "Well, if you'd just cooperated in the first place—"

"This is my room. I don't have to cooperate. Now get out before I throw you out."

"Not without my ring."

Emma knelt beside him and began gathering up scraps of paper that had fallen beneath the desk.

"I can do it," Charlie insisted. "Just go before you mess up anything else."

"There isn't anything else to mess up in here. This place is an absolute pigsty." Emma paused a moment, then added calmly. "Oh, and by the way—very smooth with Val down there. First you ask her to the dance, and then you treat her like a leper."

"I asked her 'cause I lost a bet. And what am I *supposed* to say to her?" Charlie was growing more irritable by the second. "It's like having *you* for a date to the dance." He bumped hard against her shoulder, nearly knocking her over. "Do you mind? Look, if we're going to the library, you'd better get dressed."

"I will as soon as I get the ring," Emma reminded him.

"Well, here it is." Charlie scooped it up and threw it at her. "And don't even think about keeping it. It's bad luck. That thing's going back in the cellar where it belongs!"

"That's exactly what I plan to do with it." Emma tucked the ring into the pocket of her robe. As she sat up straighter, she noticed what looked like a photograph lying beneath one corner of the bed, and she stretched over to grab it.

"Hey, what's this?" she asked.

Charlie didn't hear her at first. He was too busy grumbling and throwing stuff back into the drawer.

Emma felt a smile spread over her lips. "Hey, Charlie," she said again, "what's this picture doing in your desk?"

This time Charlie heard her. In fact, she could see the telltale rise of color in his cheeks before he even turned fully to face her.

Emma's smile widened. She was staring down at a photograph of Val, one she remembered having taken at the beach last summer. Val in her two-piece suit which left little to the imagination—Val with her golden tan and flowing hair and model-perfect smile. She held the photo up with a tantalizing little wave, but Charlie snatched it from her hand.

"So what's this doing here, Charlie?" Emma asked again. "How come you have this picture of Val?"

Charlie had that funny, helpless look of desperation—like part of him wanted to slug her, and the other part simply wanted to drop off the face of the earth. Just as Emma knew he would, he squinted his eyes at the photo, adamantly shook his head, and tossed it back to her.

"I don't know. I don't know how this got in here."

"Right. I bet you don't."

He was trying so hard to be cool and casual, but his cheeks flushed hotter. Emma fixed him with a level stare.

"How long have you had a crush on Val?"

"You're delusional." Charlie shrugged his shoulders and turned away from her, sauntering back over to his bed. He flopped down and picked up his headphones. "I haven't looked in that drawer in months. So next time you try to plant something in my room, make sure you put it in a place I'll actually see it."

Emma nodded in mock seriousness. "Oh. I get it. *I'm* the one who hid the picture there."

"You or Val," Charlie said innocently. "God, when are you two gonna grow up?"

He clamped the headphones snugly in place. Emma watched him for a moment, then slipped the photo back into the bottom drawer, beneath the crumpled papers, loose change, and old baseball cards.

"I'll be ready in fifteen minutes!" she yelled, but

Charlie was making a great show of ignoring her. After a moment's indecision, she decided to spare his pride and stop teasing him. She went to her room to get dressed.

Yet almost immediately her strange mood returned. Not even another shower or her favorite blue sweater could shake the eerie feeling of doom that hung over her. She was sure her hair still smelled faintly of smoke, though she'd practically scrubbed her scalp off. She felt restless and on edge . . . and she couldn't stop thinking about Daniel.

Emma stood in front of her mirror and frowned at her reflection. She put a cautious hand to the glass, wondering why the person looking back at her seemed like someone she didn't know.

Very slowly she slipped the ring onto her finger.

Was it only her imagination? Or had her reflection wavered just then, ever so slightly, as though the Emma she recognized was trying to fade away?

12

⁕

"I'll pick you up at five," Charlie said, stopping his car in front of the library. "Just wait for me out here."

Emma frowned at him. "I thought you were gonna help me."

"I am. We can cover more ground if we split up. I'm gonna check out the archives at the newspaper office."

"But we don't even know what year to look for."

"Well, we know it happened a long time ago, right? The girl who looked like you was wearing a long dress, and she had to escape on horseback. I'll see if I can find anything about fires on the Farmington property."

He pulled away from the curb, watching Emma in the rearview mirror, her reflection growing smaller as he drove off. He'd never admit it to her, but there was a lingering scent of smoke inside the car, and it was creeping him out. Not like the cigarette smoke he tried so hard to get rid of after he and his buddies cruised sometimes on the weekends. More like fire-smoke, the kind that came from a burning building. He'd smelled it in Emma's hair earlier. He'd told himself he was just imagining it.

In spite of the car's warm interior, Charlie shivered. He hadn't felt quite like himself since Emma's weird experience at the Farmington house, since he'd had that terrible dream about it last night. Even recalling it now sent a chill through him. It had seemed so real—everything about it, so tragic and so real—and when he thought Emma'd been in danger . . .

Charlie glanced down at his hands, surprised to see them tremble. He swerved the car into a fast-food drive-through and ordered a large coffee, black. Then he parked in a far corner of the lot and sat there with the engine idling.

What was wrong with him, anyway? Emma was the emotional one, not him; Emma was the one with the wild imagination, not him. Ever since Dad died, he'd taken it upon himself to be the man of the house, the strong one, the wise and sensible and dependable one. Mom had to be able to count on someone, and it sure couldn't be Emma, not with all her crazy ideas.

Which was why he couldn't let himself believe all this nonsense of Emma's now, Charlie told himself firmly, why he couldn't allow himself to get sucked into all these theatrics of hers. That whole fire thing had just been a nightmare, nothing more, 'cause she'd been so scared about spending the night at the house next door. And he'd been really tired last night, had slept really deeply . . . and that's the only reason he'd been drawn so far into her dream. . . .

Charlie frowned and braced himself for a sip of hot coffee.

Was he losing his touch? Were his psychic talents slipping? This was twice now in one week that Emma's dreams had totally disrupted his nights. And what about breakfast the other morning when Emma'd cornered him about Val? Remembering the scene made him squirm all over again. He'd adored Val for as long as he'd known her . . . she was the most beautiful girl he'd ever laid eyes on . . . but she was his sister's best friend, for God's sake—how dangerous and embarrassing was that? Just thinking about all the ways he'd envisioned Val—he and Val together—made his whole body suddenly rage hot. He couldn't afford to be careless like that again. If Emma ever tuned into any of those fantasies . . .

Gulping more coffee, Charlie yelped as it scalded his tongue. Quickly he set his cup down and covered his mouth with his hand.

The truth was, he was totally freaked out by all this. Freaked out by Emma's experience, by his own dream, by how he'd thought Emma was dying in the fire. He'd come out of his nightmare in a cold sweat, in a major panic attack, and he'd run straight out of the house to get to her. He'd been confused and disoriented, he'd known it was a dream, yet at the same time he'd been so certain it was real. He'd never expected to react that way. He'd never thought about Emma dying before. He'd spent his whole life wishing she weren't such a pain, wishing she'd just keep her stupid thoughts to herself and leave him alone, and then he'd seen her trapped in the fire, and he'd been desperate to save her.

Not that he could have.

Just like he couldn't save Dad from the cancer, just like he couldn't save Mom from the heartaches and the bills and the unexpected way their life had turned out.

But losing Emma . . .

Charlie leaned forward and rested his forehead on the steering wheel. A muscle clenched tight in his jaw, and he realized he was trying not to cry.

He'd never thought about losing Emma before. It seemed different somehow from losing a friend or even family, though Emma was certainly both.

Losing Emma . . .

Losing Emma would be like losing half of himself.

Charlie took a deep slow breath. Tears stung his eyes, and he felt stupid and weak and just like a little boy again, and he hated that.

"Not cool," Charlie whispered. "Definitely not cool."

He roused himself and peered out the window. He couldn't believe he was sitting out here in a parking lot getting all weird and worked up over something that wasn't even real.

"Next thing you know, I'll be as crazy as Emma," he muttered to himself.

He swigged the last of his coffee, ignoring the pain as it burned down his throat. Then he sat up straight, squared his shoulders, and peeled recklessly out of the parking lot.

13

Emma stood on the sidewalk in front of the library.

Everything looked so normal here. Pale sunlight streamed down through the bare trees overhead, speckling the pavement and dancing over the red and gold leaves at her feet. All around her, people strolled by, taking their time, talking and laughing. *Like they don't have a single care in the world,* Emma thought with a pang of envy, *like they never have nightmares that totally freak them out.* Traffic moved past her on the street, and customers went in and out of the drugstore on the corner, and she could smell the warm fragrance of cappuccino from the sidewalk café across the boulevard. Here, last night's terrifying experience seemed nothing more than what Charlie had called it—a dream. A distant, disappearing dream . . .

Yet the ring on her hand was real.

She'd kept it hidden in her pocket on the way over,

but as soon as Charlie'd left, she'd taken it out and slipped it on her finger. *Why are you even doing this? Charlie's right—it can't be anything but bad luck.*

Emma frowned, tracing the delicate outline of the heart. The truth was, she didn't really know why she was doing it. The ring intrigued her . . . frightened her . . . yet at the same time she couldn't stop thinking about it. Each time she touched it, she felt a weird flutter in the pit of her stomach, a weird sort of confusion in her head. Like she was supposed to know something, or remember something, that she couldn't quite reach.

It made her think of the dream again, and the house, and the fire . . .

And Daniel.

Gently Emma twisted the thin gold band. A faint smile came to her lips, and as a passerby accidentally jostled her, she looked up in surprise.

How long have I been standing here? I've got work to do.

She glanced at her watch, shocked to see that a half hour had already passed. Hurrying up the wide stone steps, she entered the library and headed straight for the reference desk.

"Excuse me," Emma greeted the woman behind the counter. "I'm looking for information about the Farmington house."

The librarian seemed glad to help. "You mean the original farmstead across town?" she answered pleasantly. "On County Lane?"

"That's the one. Oh, and if you have anything on the history of Hartville, that'd be good, too."

"I'm sure we must have something." The woman smiled. "Just let me go check."

"Thanks."

The woman promptly disappeared into a small adjoining office, leaving Emma alone at the desk. Leaning back against the counter, she let her eyes sweep through the room, over the worn carpet, the crammed bookshelves, framed pictures of long-dead authors, students nodding off here and there over boring research assignments. It seemed uncomfortably warm in here; it smelled even mustier than usual. Emma rubbed her nose and tried not to cough, wishing the librarian would hurry. Impatiently she continued her inspection of the room but as her gaze reached the far corner, it suddenly stopped. The Miss Lobergs were standing not twenty feet away. Side by side, heads bent together, speaking in whispers. They seemed very intent on some important, private discussion, but Emma couldn't keep herself from staring.

She'd always regarded the two women with a mixture of fear and fascination. And though she'd never admit it to Val, she'd *also* heard they killed stray animals and ate little children for breakfast.

One sister was at least six feet tall, solemn and dignified, with snowy-white hair pulled back in a perfect bun and not one strand out of place. Gold barrettes were pinned at odd angles around her head, and she always wore a dainty magnifying glass on a gold chain about her neck. The other sister, a good foot and a half shorter, was plump and animated and waved her hands in the air as she talked. Her long silver hair frizzed out in all directions, and Emma had never seen her in anything but long purple jumpers and big heavy workboots, no matter the weather or season. Today the taller sister was bundled in a sleek, black coat, the shorter one in a purple cape, and both of them wore strange-looking hats with feathers.

As Emma continued to stare, both sisters suddenly turned and looked at her. Quickly she averted her gaze but not before seeing the tall one point at her. The short one began wringing her hands. Emma moved deliberately away from them, but their whispers seemed to grow louder.

"Are you all right?"

Emma started as the librarian gave her a concerned frown.

"Oh. Sure. Sorry, my mind was someplace else."

"I think these books might have some of the history you're looking for. Feel free to make notes or copies, but unfortunately, you can't check them out."

"Thanks again; I really appreciate it."

She glanced at the corner, but the Miss Lobergs had disappeared. Still feeling unsettled, Emma hurried to a cubicle and sat down. It surprised her to discover the town could actually boast a halfway interesting past. In a matter of minutes she was eagerly scanning the small stack of books from the library's private collection. Apparently Hartville had been quite a booming riverport in its day, famous for its tobacco crops, and as Emma continued reading, she discovered that the wealthiest man in town had been none other than Josiah Farmington.

Josiah, it seemed, had owned the richest tobacco fields in the county, and the town itself had been founded by his great-great grandfather, who'd named the town after his beloved wife, Samantha Hart, as a wedding gift.

Emma kept reading, scribbling information in the notebook she'd brought with her. As she neared the end of the book and turned the last page, she let out a whisper of surprise.

There it was, in faded black and white.

A photograph of the Farmington house.

Even though the picture was blurry and had been taken from a great distance, Emma recognized it at once. The house was just like she'd always imagined it— so grand and so stately, rising up among shade trees, surrounded by wildflowers and rolling countryside. There were no other houses around it, no high iron fence— only a tidy assortment of outbuildings here and there, ripe orchards and gardens, a well, a barn, and lush fields stretching off toward the horizon. A curved driveway led up from the main road, past the barnyard and up a gentle incline to the front of the house, where a carriage was parked and waiting.

Emma stared at the carriage for a long time.

She shifted uncomfortably in her chair.

It really was hot in here, and that awful musty smell was beginning to give her a headache. She could feel it in her nose and the back of her throat, like a coating of old dust. It was getting almost hard to breathe.

She refocused her attention on the photograph in front of her, on the beautiful house, on the carriage in the drive . . .

She twisted the ring on her finger.

Yes . . . she thought to herself, *yes . . . that's where Daniel always parks the carriage . . . for my afternoon outing. . . .*

Tracing a fingertip over the picture, Emma stared until the image was nothing more than a blur. *Daniel's not in the photograph . . . of course Father would forbid it . . . but Daniel's hitched up our carriage, just like he always does at two o'clock every afternoon—*

Emma cried out as her notebook hit the floor.

She hadn't realized she'd been resting her elbow on it, unconsciously scooting it closer to the edge of the desk. She stared at it now, where it lay open at her feet.

"Our carriage," she whispered.

A frown spread slowly across her face. *Our carriage? Why'd I just say that?*

She couldn't stop staring at the notebook. Her shoulders were slumped, and she felt sluggish, as though she'd just woken up. *I must have dozed off for a second. I think I might have been dreaming—but what was it about?*

Rousing herself, she glanced up at the clock on the wall. *Two hours?* It seemed impossible that so much time had passed since she'd first sat down. Her headache was getting worse. Her eyes ached as though she'd been reading for days. Leaning over, she retrieved the notebook, then concentrated once more on the picture in the book.

There were people in the photo—she could see them now—several people standing on the top step of the wraparound porch that adorned the house. A very old man, several other men of varying ages dressed in dirty work clothes, and a plump young woman in starched apron and cap, probably a maid or a cook. The caption beneath it read: JOSIAH FARMINGTON, FAR LEFT.

Emma felt prickles along her spine. The man was dressed completely in black, standing ramrod straight and a distance apart from the others—but besides that, it was impossible to make out any details. She marked the page with a slip of paper, then went on to the other volumes.

The rest of her stack proved to be disappointing. Nothing else was even mentioned about the Farmington house or the man who'd owned it, so Emma made a copy of the photograph and returned the books to the librarian.

By now it was nearly five. She glanced uneasily around the library, but saw no further sign of the Miss Lobergs. Relieved, she let herself outside and heard Charlie honking at her from the curb.

"Did you find anything?" Emma asked, scooting in beside him. She could see some papers scattered over the backseat, and Charlie was frowning down at another bunch in his hand.

"Take a look at these," he said solemnly. "And notice the date, while you're at it."

From the tone of his voice, Emma was almost afraid to. She could see at once they were photocopies of old newspaper articles, a series of headlines from the turn of the century. LOCAL WOMAN MISSING; TRAGEDY STRIKES FARMINGTON HOUSE; FATHER MOURNS KIDNAPPED DAUGHTER.

"Kidnapped daughter?" Emma whispered.

Charlie nodded. "Her name was Emma. She was seventeen years old."

"But . . . I don't understand." Emma's hands had begun to tremble. She glanced at Charlie, but he nudged her to keep reading.

There was only one photograph, and the quality was very poor. It was a distant shot and showed an area of smoldering rubble—the ruins of the barn, Emma assumed—far off behind the house. Several men stood by, one of them resembling Josiah, but they were too far away to tell. The articles reported how Josiah Farmington had returned home this particular night to find his barn in flames, his house ransacked of money and jewelry, his firearms stolen, and his beloved daughter missing. From the battered condition of Emma's bedroom, and from the blood and scraps of clothing found there, it was obvious that a fierce struggle had taken place, evidence that Emma had probably been harmed and taken against her will.

"I don't believe this," Emma said angrily. "Emma Farmington wasn't kidnapped—Josiah *killed* her, for God's sake!"

"Yeah, well, if you were Josiah, wouldn't you wanna cover up your dirty little secret?"

"You mean, he went back inside and trashed Emma's room and tore up her clothes and sprinkled some blood around for special effects?" Emma's look was incredulous. "I don't believe it. He couldn't have gotten away with it."

"Of course he could. This was a hundred years ago, remember? And as bad as that fire probably was, there wouldn't have been any bodies left to find. Not a trace of evidence."

"But wouldn't someone have investigated? Wouldn't *someone* have suspected?"

Charlie raised an eyebrow. "With Josiah Farmington as prominent as he was, are you kidding? Em, he owned the whole town. Even if someone *did* actually suspect him, who'd have had the guts to say so?"

Leaning over, he took the articles from Emma. Then he glanced quickly through the pile, reshuffled them, and put a different page on top.

"See here? Josiah tells the sheriff he knows who did it. He tells him all about this stablehand they have—this guy who just shows up one day, dirty and hungry and needing a job."

"Daniel," Emma mumbled, and Charlie nodded.

"He tells the sheriff how he's never trusted this Daniel Frye 'cause he has an 'evil look about him,' and Farmington's always been afraid the guy might steal the family silver or murder them in their beds. He says he should have fired Daniel long ago, only he felt it was his 'God-given duty' to try to 'help poor sinners' and 'lead stray lambs back to the fold.'"

Emma felt sick to her stomach. "And of course the sheriff believed him."

"Like I said, the man was feared and respected—he probably owned the sheriff, too, for that matter. The paper says they have this huge manhunt—it goes on for weeks and weeks, they search six whole counties, but Daniel's never found."

"Is there a picture of Daniel?"

"I couldn't find any."

Emma grew silent. She could feel tears welling in her eyes, and she swallowed them down, all too aware of Charlie watching.

"It's just . . . I can't stand to think that everyone believed Josiah's story. That he got away with cold-blooded murder and blamed it all on Daniel, and the whole time he's pretending to be this devoted father. And nobody ever knew!"

"A lot of people back then got away with murder," Charlie said philosophically. "They didn't have all that forensics stuff like they do now, and this was a rural town."

"But what about the servants? Josiah had people working for him—surely they must have seen or heard something! They must have *known* what kind of person he was!"

"Look, things just weren't talked about then like they are now," Charlie reminded her. "And if the servants suspected anything, they wouldn't have risked their jobs by gossiping. They were probably all afraid of him, too."

Emma considered this. Finally she asked, "So you think the bodies weren't even found? Weren't even buried?"

"I don't know. Probably not."

"And you think maybe that's why you and I had that . . . that weird experience last night? 'Cause we're supposed to let people know about this murder?"

"I don't know that, either." For a long while Charlie said nothing. Then he slowly reached over and pointed at something on the paper. "Read the date."

"I did."

"No, I mean the actual day. See it? The fire happened in November, exactly one hundred years ago. And the anniversary of the fire is *two days* from now, Em."

Emma's breath caught in her throat. As she followed the direction of Charlie's finger, she could see the numbers printed there in black and white.

Charlie hesitated, biting his lower lip. Then he turned several of the pages over.

"There's something else. A year later, on the exact day of Emma's disappearance, Josiah Farmington suddenly dies. The paper says he committed suicide. Grief-stricken over his missing daughter, the old man hangs himself."

"Grief-stricken!" Emma burst out indignantly. "I don't believe that for one—"

"Wait. Look at this."

More photographs. Two separate close-ups of father and daughter, each one displayed side by side.

Emma stared down, saying nothing. The old man looked just as she remembered—mean, cruel, unforgiving. She could feel hate rising inside her at the very sight of him—hate so fierce and raging that it boiled up into her chest and burned at her heart.

And then she saw the young woman beside him.

The young Miss Emma Farmington.

Again Emma's hands trembled dangerously. The face staring back at her was almost frightening in its familiarity, the same face she saw every morning when she brushed her teeth and combed her hair and talked to herself in the bathroom mirror.

As if from a great distance, she felt Charlie's hand on her shoulder.

"It's incredible," Charlie murmured. "She looks just like you."

14

The hair was different, of course. The girl in the picture had her hair swept back in a loose bun, soft tendrils spilling down over the high lace collar of her black dress, the rest held in place with combs. She wore no makeup; her expression was formal and somewhat strained, yet Emma recognized it now for what it really was—a deep-worn sadness and fear.

Without thinking, she twisted the ring on her finger.

She smiled almost tenderly at the photograph.

"I was always afraid of him," she mumbled to Charlie. "He threatened me . . . beat me sometimes. Locked me in my room for days at a time with nothing to eat. He was insanely possessive. That's why he hated Daniel so much, you know. Because he knew I was in love with him."

She closed her eyes briefly . . . opened them again.

Charlie was staring at her with a startled expression on his face.

"Jeez, Em," he said sharply. "Knock it off." He grabbed the papers from her hands, tossed them in the back, and started the car.

Now Emma looked surprised. "What?"

"Don't you think you're carrying this thing a little too far?"

"What do you mean?"

"I mean, quit talking like you're *her*. You're *not* her."

For an instant Emma felt a rush of confusion. "Did I say *I*? I *meant* her. I don't know why I said that. I didn't mean to say that."

"And anyway, you don't know anything about that girl's private life—what it was really like between her and her father. Quit making stuff up—it's too weird."

"But I didn't mean to," Emma said again. "I don't know why I said that—it just seemed to be true." She paused, then added defensively, "Well, how else *could* it have been, Charlie? I mean, he locked her in the barn and let her die."

"Em, just shut up." Charlie turned his full attention to his driving. He didn't say another word all the way home. It wasn't till they'd pulled into the driveway that Emma spoke to him again.

"You're doing it, Charlie—acting like a jerk 'cause you're scared. Just 'cause we can't explain it, and we don't understand it. And 'cause that girl looks like me."

"Don't even start," Charlie warned her. "I mean, if you wanna talk about scared, let me remind you *who* begged me to hide that ring so you wouldn't—"

He broke off as Emma tried to tuck her hand quickly into her pocket.

"And now you're wearing it again." Charlie hit both palms against the steering wheel. "I don't believe this. What are you—crazy?"

He slammed the car door and stomped up the drive to the house. After a moment, Emma gathered up all the papers and followed him in.

"I saw the Miss Lobergs at the library." She frowned at the memory and dropped her stuff on the kitchen table. "It was weird. They were huddled together, and it was like they were talking about me."

"Everybody does, you know," Charlie retorted blandly. "You're so important, they just can't help themselves."

Emma ignored the sarcasm. "I have to go back for my things," she reminded him as he grabbed a handful of cookies and crammed half of them into his mouth.

Charlie spoke around oatmeal and raisins. "So go."

"You said you'd come with me."

"I can't." He shuddered dramatically from head to toe. "I'm too scared!"

Scowling, he bounded up the stairs to his room, leaving Emma staring angrily after him.

Charlie *was* scared. He was every bit as spooked as she was—she could sense the unease he was struggling to keep hidden. The thought of what she'd said back there in the car totally unnerved her now—the way she'd spoken in the first person, just as if she were Emma Farmington, just as if she knew things only Emma Farmington would know.

Reluctantly she looked down at the heart-shaped ring. Some instinct warned her to take it off now, to get rid of it before this whole strange thing went any further.

But she couldn't.

As strong as that instinct was, there was something even more powerful inside of her, some compelling emotion she couldn't ignore, almost a yearning to keep it on her finger where it fit so perfectly and looked so right.

Emma glanced up the staircase. She could hear Charlie's music going full-blast, and a fresh surge of anger went through her. *Fine.* She didn't need Charlie to go back with her to the house—she knew right where her things were, and she wouldn't have to waste time searching for them. *In and out, what could be more simple?*

Except she wished she'd gone earlier in the day, while the sun had still been out in all its winter brightness, and the breeze had seemed more playful than cruel.

I wonder if anything's left of that barn?

The thought came to her as she carefully scaled the fence between the two properties. She remembered from the book in the library that the barn had appeared more to the foreground of the photograph, some distance from the main house and far off to the right of it, somewhere clearly down the street from the Donovans' front yard. Emma narrowed her gaze, scanning the woods that crept right up to the Farmington fence in back, tree limbs reaching through, ivy crawling over, as though nature couldn't wait to devour the old place. She hurried on, wishing it had, and long before now. Before she'd moved in next door . . . before she'd had the dream . . .

She tried to shut her mind against the memory. *The barn . . . the flames . . . Daniel's body beneath me . . .*

Emma walked faster. Her mind filled with vivid

images of Josiah's rage and Daniel impaled on the pitchfork. How he'd staggered backward, clutching at his chest, how she'd thrown herself across him and prayed to die so they could always be together.

"This is crazy. I've got to stop thinking about all this stuff."

She was out of breath and sweating in spite of the cold, and as she hurried along the porch, she could see the gaping hole where she'd fallen through the night before. The sky wasn't totally dark yet. Twilight oozed through the trees and the long tangled vines, settling itself uneasily around the eaves of the old house.

Emma stepped closer to the hole. She stood for a long moment, gazing down into the shadows, wishing she'd thought to bring a flashlight. A bundle that looked like her sleeping bag had rolled off several feet from where she'd fallen, and the contents of her backpack lay scattered across the floor. She closed her eyes, drew a deep breath, then opened them again. The warped floorboards groaned slightly beneath her weight, and she hastily made for the front door.

Now . . . if I can just remember the way to the cellar. . . .

The door swung easily at her touch. *Not like last time, when it wouldn't let me out. . . .* After a moment's hesitation she stepped cautiously across the threshold, then stood listening in the cavernous gloom. Nothing had changed since yesterday—not the coating of dust and cobwebs, not the smell of mold and decay. And yet something *was* different, she could sense it—something she couldn't see or even hear—something still and silent and watchful, holding its breath beyond the shadows, waiting and curious.

Emma could feel goose bumps along her arms . . . shivers down her spine. Her whole body felt as if a low volt of electricity was pumping through it, from her head to the very tips of her toes. Her heart began to race. She could feel cold sweat on her brow, and her knees suddenly threatened to give out.

She turned slowly, her gaze riveted to one spot in the corner. A corner much darker than the others, a darkness with shape and form and intensity and something even more frightening—*awareness—awareness and intelligence*—something *human,* something *alive*—

Emma's heart leaped.

The darkness was moving now—pulling itself from the other shadows surrounding it, coming away from the wall and toward the very spot where she was standing.

There was purpose to its movement.

There was familiarity.

As a cry caught in Emma's throat, she saw the face at last, the midnight eyes, the arms reaching out to hold her.

"Emma," he said. "I knew you'd come."

15

She loved the smell of him.

The raw, earthy smell of him as she pressed her face to his chest, to the threadbare fabric of his shirt, the smell of long work and outdoors, a man comfortable with who he was and would always be.

Emma buried her face against him and breathed deeply. She loved the feel of his hand stroking the back of her hair, his body pressed hard against hers. She could hear the racing of his heart, feel its wild rhythm beating in time to her own, and she smiled and hugged him tighter.

Very gently he slid his fingers beneath her chin. He tilted her head upward and gazed deep into her eyes. She saw the love there, the pure absolute love there, and it made her want to cry, such a perfect reflection of the love she felt for him.

His head began to lower. His lips tenderly brushed hers. He pulled back a little and gave her that smile, and her heart melted within her.

"May I have this dance?" he asked. His voice was deep and strong and sure of itself. He made a mocking bow, and she pulled back, horrified.

"You know you shouldn't be with me in the house. Father will be home any minute—he'll be furious if he finds you here!"

"I'm the only one he trusts with that horse he's so proud of. Yet I'm not good enough for his daughter." Daniel laughed and circled her waist with one arm. "Don't worry. In that old carriage of his we'll hear him in plenty of time. Besides, it's Betsey's day off, and it'd be a sin to waste it. Come, Emma, dance with me."

Before she could protest, he led her in a dizzying waltz, around and around and around, through the hallway, into the front parlor, till she was laughing and out of breath. The glow of the fireplace softened the formal austerity of the room—the stiff horsehair sofa and straight-backed chairs, the carved tables of darkly polished wood, neatly ordered shelves of leather-bound books, the stern portraits of Farmington ancestors staring down in mute disapproval from the walls. A porcelain clock kept rigid time upon the mantel, but Daniel's voice drowned it out as he hummed their own tune, swooping and dipping and gliding, laughing at Emma's happiness, dancing faster and faster, till they both collapsed in a heap before the fire.

For a long moment they simply lay there, side by side, trying to catch their breath. There was no music now, no sound at all, save for the clock and the crackling of the flames and the soft hiss of falling ash.

Emma turned her head to look at him. His face was only inches from hers, and his eyes seemed to draw her into his very soul.

Very slowly he raised himself on one elbow.

With his free hand, he took the combs from her hair. He loosened the bun at the back of her neck, spilling her hair around her shoulders. His eyes never left her face. She could feel his breath, faint and warm, upon her cheek, and she could feel his fingertips as they slid down the side of her face, down the side of her neck, as they lingered at the tiny pearl buttons of her dress and began to unfasten them, one by one.

"I love you," she whispered. "Oh, God, Daniel, I love you so much."

It was an unbearable ache inside her. As Daniel's body shifted, his hands caught each side of her face, and he kissed her deeply, desperately, his lips melting into hers. She could feel the passion; it was more intense with every second, over her eyelids, her cheeks, tracing a pathway down her neck, burning her soft bare skin.

"Let me take you." Daniel's voice was husky with emotion, and she clasped her arms tightly around his neck and drew him even closer. "Let me take you away from here, Emma—someplace he'll never be able to hurt you again."

And she was crying, and he was kissing away her tears, and somewhere, far off in the distance, yet alarmingly close—*too close!*—came the sound of creaking carriage wheels and the whinny of a horse eager to be home.

Emma choked on a scream. For one horrible second the two of them pulled apart and stared into each other's eyes, where the love and the longing turned abruptly to pain.

"You must go," Emma whispered. "He'll be looking for you outside, he'll expect you to be there."

Yet every fiber of her being yearned for him to stay. With one deft movement Daniel was on his feet, pulling her up beside him. He kissed her once more, roughly, before turning and disappearing through the back of the house.

Emma spun just as quickly and started for the stairs. Her fingers worked frantically at her buttons, then she nervously gathered her hair back from her flushed cheeks. *The combs!* Daniel had dropped them on the floor by the fire, yet even now she could hear the ponderous tread of her father's boots on the front porch, pausing just outside the door as he growled one last order to his lowly stableboy.

Emma dashed upstairs. She heard the slam of the front door just as she pushed her own door quietly shut.

My sanctuary . . .

For that's how she'd come to think of this room—the only room in the house—that was truly her own. A peaceful retreat where she could think, where she could dream her most private dreams. A safe place, a sweet place to hide. There was not the slightest touch of her father in here, not in the faded roses of the wallpaper or the soft lace of the curtains or even the gilded oval mirror that had once been her mother's.

Emma sat on her bed and trembled now, one hand at her mouth to hold back a sob. She heard her father coming up the stairs toward her room, and she hurriedly situated herself at her dressing table.

His knock echoed like a gunshot.

Taking a deep breath to compose herself, Emma managed a weak, "Come in."

The suspicion was there, of course, written over every craggy line of his face. His narrowed eyes swept the room with a glance, and he walked up behind her, holding her reflection mercilessly in her mirror.

"Are you ill, Daughter?" he asked.

Emma responded with a halfhearted nod. She put her fingertips to her temples. "Yes, my head's been aching since morning. I thought it would pass, but it only seems to have grown worse. Did you finish all your business in town, Father?"

If Josiah Farmington heard the question, he gave no sign. "Well," he mused, "perhaps the pain comes from harboring sinful thoughts."

The cold serpent eyes narrowed even more. Emma's fingers pressed so tightly against her head that a sudden wave of dizziness swept over her.

"I harbor no sinful thoughts, Father," she answered calmly. "How could I, with all the good you've taught me? Now, Betsey's left a roast chicken for dinner— would you like to eat, or will you rest first?"

One gnarled hand slid slowly down her hair. "And where are your combs? The ones you had on this morning at breakfast."

"Oh." Emma's heart jolted in her chest, yet her voice was unperturbed. "I must have left them in the parlor when I was sewing earlier. My head hurt so badly, I had to take them out."

Turning suddenly, Emma looked up and fixed her father with a tender smile. The simple gesture caught him off guard, as she knew it would. He hesitated, as though searching for more suspicions, then gave a curt nod.

"I'll have a nap first."

"Very well, Father."

She turned back to her mirror. She waited as he walked out into the hallway. Then she covered her face with her hands and leaned forward onto the table.

It was the door that frightened her.

The door slamming suddenly, violently, shuddering the very boards beneath her feet.

Emma gasped and jumped back. For a split second there was nothing but total blackness around her, but then, as her eyes began to focus, she felt an icy chill run through her veins.

She didn't know where she was.

The room around her was cold and silent, as still and dark as death. There was no furniture of any kind, and the sound of her breathing echoed loudly in the emptiness.

Emma stood there, rooted to the floor.

She glanced over her shoulder and saw a gaping doorway, and somehow she knew that it opened onto an upstairs hall, and that if she walked out and turned to the left, there would be steps leading back down. . . .

How'd I get here?

She had absolutely no memory of climbing the staircase or finding her way to this room at the very end of the corridor.

"This can't be real," Emma whispered. She pulled the sleeves of her sweater down over her wrists; she clamped her arms tightly around her chest. "This can't be happening."

The very thought of wandering through this house completely unnerved her. The thought of having come to this room she never knew existed, of having come through no choice of her own, as though she were *meant* to come, as though she *belonged*.

She screamed as another crash resounded through the house. *The door—someone slammed the door!* For a minute her mind flashed back, and her hands went nervously to her head, searching for—*what?*—something she'd forgotten—something she'd left downstairs—yet almost at the same instant she *knew* it wasn't a door slamming, not a door at all. It was only the tree outside the window, the tree in the cold restless wind, pounding against the side of this upstairs room.

Emma pressed both hands to her forehead. *What's wrong with me—I must be losing my mind!*

The room spun around her.

As she turned to run, she saw a young woman near the window, a young woman staring back, her eyes equally wild with terror.

And then, suddenly, Emma burst out laughing.

It was a laugh bordering on hysteria, but a laugh nonetheless. She gazed at the far wall, at the grimy mirror that hung there, reflecting her own frightened face. She let out a sigh of relief and instinctively clutched her stomach, willing the queasiness to pass.

The mirror was so old and warped, her face scarcely looked human. *More like a mask,* Emma thought, as she went closer to examine it. A pale, wavy mask flecked with black scabs, like something long dead and decayed.

I sat here and looked at my face, because he loved me, because he thought I was beautiful. . . .

She remembered, then.

The dancing, his kisses, the warm strong feel of him, every sight and sound, every raw emotion. *Real.* Every bit as real as standing here now, as real as this room, as this wall, as this oval of antique glass.

Emma gazed deep into her own sad eyes.

She held their sorrowful gaze until she noticed a faint movement behind her in the mirror . . . as though a shadowy figure had stepped forward into the room.

Gasping, she spun toward the door.

The room was empty; the hallway beyond was deserted.

With her heart pounding, Emma faced the mirror once more.

And still that faint wavering of shadow reflected behind her . . . while in the heavy silence of the room, a deep mournful sigh seemed to echo softly from every corner. . . .

"Daniel?" she murmured.

If she stared hard enough, she could almost see a face looking back at her through the gloom, a young man with coal black hair and midnight eyes.

And if she held her breath, if she listened closely in the eerie quiet, she could almost hear him whispering, *"Emma . . . Emma . . . please come back to me."*

16

〜🙰〜

"*E*mma . . ."

From some faraway distance Charlie thought he heard a voice.

Frowning, he sat up from his stack of pillows and lifted one side of his headphones. The volume was so loud, his head felt as if it might come right off—but how else was he supposed to deal with his crazy sister?

He'd stood at his bedroom window earlier and watched Emma leave, watched her climb the fence and go off alone to the Farmington house. He'd made up his mind he wasn't going to help her this time, no matter what happened. He couldn't believe how obsessed she was getting with this stupid dream of hers, and how she'd acted so weird in the car coming back from the library—how she'd sat right there beside him, talking as if she were that *other* Emma person from the past.

He'd almost stopped the car and jumped out, it had unnerved him so much. Not that he'd ever admit it, not to her or anyone else.

Now Charlie scowled and clamped his headphones back in place. Slouching down on the corner of his bed, he closed his eyes and drummed his hands on his knees in time to the music.

"Emma . . ."

He bolted upright, his scowl deepening. There it was again, that voice, only it sounded more insistent this time. *Jeez, am I going crazy, too?* After all, he and Emma had shared everything else throughout their lives—flu, poison ivy, chicken pox, even pneumonia once. *So why not insanity, too,* Charlie thought wryly.

He switched off the music. He flung his headphones onto his desk and listened, but the house was eerily silent.

"Mom?" he called softly. She'd been asleep in her room when they'd gotten home, but maybe she'd set her alarm early for some reason. Tiptoeing down the hall, he cracked open her door and peeked in. "Mom?"

His mother didn't move. Charlie stood there and watched her for several minutes, then quietly pulled her door shut. *I'm losing it.* He ran both hands back through his hair and gave a loud groan. *Great. Whatever Emma's got, she's infected me with it.*

He felt restless and uneasy. He wandered back to his room and paused beside his desk. He stared down at the papers scattered there—all the research he and Emma had done on the house next door. Reluctantly he picked them up and started sorting through them again for the—*how many times is it now? I can't even remember.* His brow furrowed in concentration. For a brief instant he actually considered going next door to check on Emma, then firmly talked himself out of it. *It's her imagination, not mine. Let her deal with it.*

Tossing the papers aside, he forced himself to take a deep breath. Very slowly, methodically, he concentrated on clearing his mind. Thought by thought . . . worry by worry . . . until it went peacefully blank. He pictured it as a calm, deep pool. He pictured a high, thick wall surrounding it. Now he could choose for himself what to let in and what to keep out. Emma had worked herself all up over this Farmington thing, and he sure wasn't going to let her ruin his evening.

"That's better," Charlie murmured. "Much better."

He decided to take a shower. He stood for a long time, letting the hot water run over him, soothing his tension away. He soaped up his face and his neck and his shoulders, and he tilted his head into the hard spray, and at first he wasn't even aware of the curious lightness spreading through him, warming the pit of his stomach, flowing along his veins. It dawned on him slowly, stealthily, almost as if he'd detached from himself, until suddenly the lightness vanished, replaced at once by something dark and heavy and cold.

Charlie frowned and rubbed the soap from his eyes. *What was I thinking about?* He couldn't recall any specific thoughts just now—certainly not anything sinister—though he couldn't be sure. All he knew was that those earlier feelings of uneasiness had returned, like some unspoken warning.

"*Emma . . .*"

Quickly he turned off the water. He stepped out of

the tub and wrapped a towel around his waist, then wiped both hands across the mirror over the sink.

His own face gazed back at him, strangely disembodied in the lingering steam of the bathroom. He looked like a pale apparition of himself, and for a split second it was almost as if his image began to melt and to change, until it was Emma's face where his own should have been.

Charlie gasped and drew back.

He grabbed a washcloth from the sink and smeared it over the glass. He saw his reflection there again, all the familiar lines and angles of it, though his expression was shaken. He could feel his heart slowing to normal rhythm. Swearing under his breath, he jerked open the bathroom door.

Someone was standing there.

With a yelp Charlie jumped back as Val stared at him with shocked eyes.

The moment stretched to eternity. Charlie's grip tightened on his towel. Val's glance swept him from head to toe. He could feel his face flaming beet red, and he looked quickly at his mother's door, expecting her to wake up and walk out.

"Oh . . . I . . ." Val motioned awkwardly toward the staircase. "The house was open. I just . . . I was . . ." Her eyes swept him again, more deliberate this time. "Was . . . you know . . . looking for Emma . . ."

Her voice trailed off. A smile played over her mouth, and her gaze focused back on his.

Charlie's flush deepened. His whole body felt hot. He pulled himself together with all the dignity and sarcasm he could muster.

"Oh. Sorry," he deadpanned, keeping his voice low. "She was abducted by aliens."

"Well, when will she be back?"

"Jeez, Val." Muttering, Charlie shoved past her into his room. "Do I look like her personal secretary?"

"You look like something," Val teased. "But definitely not a personal secretary."

Charlie was still grumbling, digging through drawers for his clothes. "My thoughts . . . my dreams . . . my room . . . now my shower . . . Can't a guy even have any privacy in his own house?" He could still feel Val watching him. He turned to face her and spread his arms wide. "See anything you'd like?" he asked dryly.

"Forget it. I don't even like anything I see." She moved toward the stairs and added, "Maybe I'll just wait for Emma to get back."

"Whatever." Charlie started to shut his door when a sudden thought came to him. "Val!" he hissed.

She paused on the top step. "What?"

"Were you calling her name when you came in?"

"Whose name?"

"Emma's. Did you yell her name when you came in?"

Val shook her head. "No. I figured your mom would be sleeping, so I just came on up here. Why?"

"No reason," Charlie mumbled.

He listened as she went down to the kitchen. Then he closed his door and sat down shakily on the end of his bed.

What's going on, Em? What's happening to us?

17

༡ༀ༢

"Where were you?" Val demanded. "I've been wait-ing for nearly an hour! Charlie said you'd been ab-ducted by aliens."

Emma stood on the back porch, gazing in through the door. Her mouth opened and closed soundlessly, and she gripped the doorknob with pale fingers.

"Hey." Val got up out of the chair and approached her cautiously. "Hey, Em, are you okay?"

Emma managed a nod. She willed herself to smile. "Yeah. Sure. Just out of breath, is all."

"Come in here! Are you crying?"

"No, silly, it's from the wind. It's getting really cold."

But Val was staring at her, unconvinced. "You're a total mess. I don't think I've ever seen you this dirty."

Emma followed Val's gaze down the front of her

sweater, her jeans, her shoes. "Well . . ." She thought quickly. "I was looking for something in the garage."

Val continued to stare. Emma fumbled with the door and pulled it shut behind her.

"The garage," Val said.

"Yeah. Looking for something."

"All this time you've been out in the garage. And Charlie didn't know? And you didn't hear me drive up?"

"Well . . ." Emma walked over to the sink and began washing her hands. She had her back to Val, but she could still feel her best friend's eyes boring into her. "I guess I was just so busy, I lost track of time. You know how I am when I'm really into something—I get obsessed."

"I didn't see a light on out there," Val persisted.

"Well, it . . . burned out. I ended up using a flashlight."

"So what were you obsessing over in your garage?"

Emma's mind raced. She stalled for time. She ran the water more loudly and glanced over her shoulder. "What?"

"I said, what were you—" Val began, but another voice cut her off.

"Hey, Em, did you find those old magazines Mom wanted?"

Both girls turned as Charlie leaned in casually from the hall. He looked as if he'd just gotten out of the shower, his hair still wet, jeans zipped but not buttoned, feet bare, arms engaged in tugging a T-shirt over his head. Val couldn't take her eyes off him.

"The *magazines*," Charlie repeated, frowning in Emma's direction. "Did you find them?"

Surprised, Emma peered back at him. *I don't believe this—Charlie's actually covering for me?* After a flustered second she stammered, "No . . . but . . . but I still have a few more boxes to go through."

"I knew you wouldn't find them," Charlie grumbled.

"I . . ." Again Emma thought quickly, playing along with his lie. "I said I wasn't finished yet. Give me a break."

Val reluctantly tore her gaze away from Charlie. "Magazines? You were obsessed over some magazines?"

"She's always obsessed about something." Charlie made a sound of disgust in his throat. "Always off somewhere in her own weird little world."

That little remark was certainly deliberate, Emma thought. She gave him a dirty look, and he shrugged innocently and swaggered away.

Val continued to watch the doorway longingly. When Charlie failed to reappear, she turned her attention back to Emma. "What magazines were you supposed to be looking for?"

"Oh, it doesn't matter—I'm tired of worrying about them. In fact, I'm just really, really tired."

Emma stood there with the dishtowel in her hands, wishing Val would go away, feeling guilty that she wished it. She felt beaten and fragile, she felt as if she'd been on some long trip and back, she felt disoriented. She wanted to talk to Charlie, yet she didn't. She wanted to go back to the house; she never wanted to go back again.

"So what do you feel like doing tonight?" Val piped up.

Emma looked at her helplessly. "Nothing," she said at last.

"Nothing?"

Again the helpless stare. Emma's mind spun wildly, yet her face remained calm. *How can I stand here like this, like everything's so normal, when I've just been in some other place, in some other time—*

"Val, honest, I still feel like I'm coming down with something. Right now I just want to go to bed."

"Well . . ." Val studied her friend closely, frowning as Emma looked away. "Maybe you're right. You don't look good at all. Though I have to say, your hair smells great. What is that?"

Emma's expression was blank. She shrugged her shoulders.

"Kind of . . . I don't know . . ." Wrinkling her nose, Val took a deep sniff. "Earthy. Natural."

"I've . . . been experimenting."

"It's great; I'll have to try it. Maybe when you feel better."

"Yes," Emma agreed, relieved. "Tomorrow, probably. Tomorrow I'll probably feel better. Thanks for understanding, Val. I mean, I wouldn't want you to come down with something 'cause of me."

Val's expression hovered between suspicion and total bewilderment. "You're really acting weird, Em," she said at last. Retrieving her keys and jacket from the kitchen table, she started slowly for the door.

"You'll call if you need anything?" she insisted.

"Sure I will. You know I will."

"Because Charlie sure won't be any help if you need it."

"No surprise there. I promise I'll call."

"You almost sound glad I'm leaving." Val frowned. "Something's going on here, I think."

"What are you talking about? Nothing's going on!" Emma clutched at the last shred of her patience and put one hand to her forehead. "I'm coming down with the flu. That's how I feel—achy and grouchy. Like the flu."

"Well . . . okay." Val opened the door and took a last glance back. "If you need me."

"I *promise*."

Again Val hesitated. Finally she said, "You can tell me anything, you know."

Biting her lip, Emma nodded. She lowered her head for a moment, then looked back up at her friend. *I wish I could, Val, but it's too crazy, even for you to believe, and anyway, it might just be me, it might just be me going completely insane—*

"I know I can, Val," Emma replied softly.

Val smiled and let herself out. The door had hardly clicked shut when Charlie made a second appearance in the doorway. He stared at her expectantly, but Emma turned her back.

"Thanks for bailing me out," she mumbled, but Charlie wasn't interested in her gratitude.

"Where've you been? And where's your stuff?"

"Answer number one—you know where I've been. Answer number two . . ." Emma sank down lamely into a chair. "I don't have it."

"Excuse me—I thought that's the whole reason you were going back there."

"It was. But something happened."

"Right." He didn't seem surprised at her announcement. Instead he walked over to the counter, leaned back against it, and folded his arms over his chest. "I'm waiting."

Emma didn't answer right away. The time she'd spent with Daniel was private and sacred, something that shouldn't be shared. Those were *their* moments—Daniel's and hers—and the thought of allowing someone else just one glimpse of them suddenly seemed the worst sort of betrayal—even if that someone *was* her twin.

"What *happened*?" Charlie pressed impatiently.

"I just . . ." Emma drew a deep breath. "I just started looking through the house. I think I found the room upstairs that belonged to Emma Farmington."

"How do you know that?"

She shrugged. "Just a feeling."

"You're not telling me everything."

Emma looked away from him. She'd never been able to lie to Charlie—not during all their years together, and certainly not now. They just knew each other too well.

"Well, there was this mirror." She'd give him that much. Otherwise he'd keep nagging at her, and she'd have to exert more energy trying to come up with something else.

"A mirror," Charlie repeated. "That's all, just a mirror? Well, what'd it do, talk to you or something? Give you a glimpse into the future?"

"It didn't do anything. I just think it probably belonged to Emma Farmington."

"And so you saw this mirror, and it put a spell on you, so you didn't bring your stuff home."

Emma shook her head. She was feeling confused again, tired and vulnerable. "I just forgot, that's all. I got sidetracked, and I just forgot."

"You were with him," Charlie said flatly.

Emma didn't answer. She stared down at the kitchen floor, and she heard Charlie let out a sigh.

"You saw him again, didn't you?" he persisted. "I couldn't see what happened, but what I felt was pretty powerful. And you're not about to share any of the details, are you?"

Still Emma said nothing. She looked up again, into her brother's narrowed eyes.

"Look, Emma, I don't know what's going on, and I don't understand what's happening, but stay away from that house," Charlie grumbled.

"I thought that house didn't scare you." Emma regarded him coolly. "I thought you didn't believe in supernatural experiences."

"It doesn't, and I don't. But you're starting to sound like a loony."

Emma bristled. "Look, it's not your problem, okay? *Or* your stuff that's still over there. So quit worrying about it."

"I guess I'll just have to go over there tomorrow and—"

"You don't have to do anything." Emma jumped up and faced him squarely. "Stay away from my house."

"*Your* house?"

Emma heard Charlie's surprised laugh as she ran from the room. She didn't stop when he called after her, and she didn't unlock her door when he banged on it to come in.

She just lay on her bed in the dark, shivering and confused, still feeling the warmth of her lover's touch.

18

❦

"Morning, Sunshine," Mrs. Donovan teased.

Emma glowered and scuffed across the kitchen floor, sniffing disinterestedly at a plate of doughnuts while she poured herself a cup of strong coffee. She took a chair opposite her mother and refocused her scowl on the newspaper lying between them.

"I hate mornings," she grumbled. "I hate Sundays. I hate knowing I have to go back to school tomorrow." She hesitated, then narrowed her eyes. "How come you're so happy?"

Mrs. Donovan looked amused. She rested both elbows on the table and regarded her daughter thoughtfully.

"I'm always happy when I get to spend time with my favorite daughter. And since you're in such a wonderful mood, do you have any idea where Charlie might have gone off to just now in such a hurry?"

"I hate Charlie," Emma said. She reached for the cream pitcher, started to pour, then changed her mind and set it back down. "I hope every girl in school suddenly thinks he's a total loser, and he never has a date for the rest of his life."

"Hmmm," her mother answered. "Somehow, I'm not convinced that will ever happen."

"Everybody thinks he's so great. Well, if we're supposed to look so much alike, how come nobody thinks *I'm* so great? How come *I* don't have guys burning up the phone lines and beating down the doors?"

"Sounds like you two must have had quite a fight."

Emma didn't answer. She dumped some sugar into her cup and gave the coffee a vigorous stir, not caring when it slopped out onto the clean placemat.

"I hear he's taking Val to the winter dance," her mother ventured cautiously.

Emma nodded.

"How about you? Have you thought about who you'd like to go with?"

Emma's head snapped up. For one second her mind blanked completely out, and she stared at her mother with unseeing eyes. *Daniel . . . waltzing me around the room . . . taking the combs from my hair . . .*

A slow rush of heat spread out from her heart, trembling through her hands.

"Emma! Watch what you're doing!"

Her mother's voice brought her back again, and Emma stared down at the overturned cup, at the scalding liquid dripping off the table and into her lap.

"Watch out!" Mrs. Donovan jumped up and made

a frantic swipe with her napkin. "Honey, are you okay?"

Emma jumped up, too, knocking her chair over backward. The bottom of her nightshirt was soaked, and her knees were red where the coffee had splashed. She stared down at them stupidly.

"Emma!" Jerking her by the elbow, Mrs. Donovan pulled her to the sink. "What on earth is the matter with you? Here—let me put some cold water on that. You could have burned your whole leg!"

"It's okay, Mom." Emma's voice was shaking almost as much as her hands. "I'm sorry—I don't know what happened—I—"

Frowning, her mother gathered her up and held her close. "You scared the life out of me!" she scolded lovingly. "*Please* be more careful—that could really have been a bad accident."

Emma nodded. She molded herself into the circle of her mother's arms and tried not to cry. She wasn't even sure what had happened just then—part of her had been here in the kitchen, and part of her had been dancing, laughing, in a flickering, firelit room. . . .

"Hold that cloth on there . . . just awhile longer," her mother ordered. "Don't you want to sit down?"

"No. Thanks, Mom. I better get dressed before something else happens." She tried to turn it into a joke, but she saw the worry in her mother's eyes. As she started upstairs, Mrs. Donovan called after her.

"By the way, Emma—have you seen the cell phone? I can't imagine where it's gone—I've looked everywhere."

Emma closed her eyes briefly. She took a deep breath. "No, Mom, but I'm sure it'll turn up somewhere. Charlie probably has it."

Charlie probably has it right now, even as we speak. Because I'll bet anything he's gone back to the Farmington place to get my stuff.

The sudden realization made her angry. She threw on some clothes and hurried back downstairs, ignoring her mother's bewildered stare.

"Emma—what on earth—"

"I'm late, Mom. I was supposed to meet Val half an hour ago—I didn't realize the time—"

"But, Emma, that burn—"

"It's fine, Mom, really! Bye!"

She slammed the door, not giving her mother a chance to answer. *Damn you, Charlie! That's my house— they're my things!* She ran for the fence, climbed over, and kept running.

Charlie wasn't anywhere outside. Emma checked all around the old house but didn't see the faintest sign of life. Peering down through the hole in the porch, she could see that her things were missing. He must have gone inside, she reasoned, and immediately let herself in the front door.

"Charlie!" she shouted. "Charlie, you have no right! Do you hear me? *No right!*"

Her voice echoed back to her in the silence. It trembled in the air for several moments, and then it faded and died.

Emma lifted her eyes to the high ceiling, to the lofty staircase, to the darkness waiting at the top.

"Charlie?" she called again. "Charlie, you'd better come out now—I'm not in the mood for jokes!"

But Charlie didn't answer. No one did. Emma felt the sudden shock of smallness and aloneness, and she backed slowly in the direction of the door.

"Charlie?"

Her voice was softer now, not nearly as angry nor as brave. She was so *sure* he'd be here—yet the house had that vast feeling of emptiness, as though no presence— not even her own—had entered here in many, many years.

A cold prickling crept along the back of her neck.

Had the shadows stirred in that corner? Restless and uneasy? She heard a mournful sigh, felt a rush of cold air, as though the entire house were settling itself around her.

"Daniel?" she whispered. "Is that you?"

"No," the voice answered softly. "He's not here right now—can I take a message?"

"*Charlie!*"

Furiously Emma swung around. Her brother fell back several steps and cupped his hands around his mouth.

"This is the Afterlife Answering Service," he announced loudly. "Just leave your name and number, and one of our friendly spirits will get back with you as soon as they can."

Emma was shaking all over, both from rage and from fear. Shoving past Charlie, she stomped out into the yard. She could hear him shouting at her, but she refused to listen. Only when the cell phone sailed past her shoulder did she stop and whirl around.

"Nice shot!" she yelled at him. "You could have hit me, you jerk!"

Charlie was lugging her backpack and sleeping bag at a leisurely pace. He shrugged off her anger and laughed.

"There are worse ways to die than death by phone,

Em. Aren't you gonna thank me for getting your stuff?"

"Why should I? I told you I'd go back for it."

"Like you did yesterday. Yeah, I remember."

Emma didn't answer. She waited for him to catch up with her, then fixed him with her fiercest scowl, which Charlie pointedly ignored.

"Okay," he said, taking her arm. "Wanna tell me what that was all about back there?"

"I don't know what you're talking about."

Charlie did a mincing imitation of his sister's voice. "Daniel! Oh, Daniel, my love! Come to me and we'll—"

"Shut up, Charlie!"

Emma tried to pull free, but Charlie tightened his hold on her.

"Calm down, will you? It's a joke!"

"Not a funny one. Like most of your jokes."

Charlie made a valiant effort to look solemn. "Okay, what do you wanna do? Hire a psychic? Call a priest? Have an exorcism?"

"You know, yesterday you almost had me believing you were serious about this. In case you've forgotten, two innocent people were murdered, and one of them looked like me *and* had my name. Call me crazy, but hey!—it *bothers* me!"

"Okay." Charlie sighed, releasing her. "Maybe it bothers me, too. There—are you happy? But each time it starts to bother me, I remind myself that it happened about a century ago!"

"Yeah, well, it also happened this past Friday, all over again. Only this time *I* was part of the action. And according to the dates on those newspapers, in exactly one day from now it'll be a hundred years since the fire.

Which does *not* make me feel particularly secure."

Charlie gave her a sidelong look. "The barn's gone, Em. Nothing's gonna happen." And then, because she didn't look convinced, he added, "It goes like this. There's some big event—some kind of tragedy, something really emotional—and the house sucks up this weird sort of energy from it. Then later, when certain conditions are the same—you know, the same date, the same kind of weather, even people who look like the ones from the past—that energy releases, and the same tragedy happens again, just like it did before. Only now it's a fantasy—a ghost story—'cause it's not real."

"And since when have you become such an authority, Einstein?"

"Well, I read about it," Charlie said defensively.

"You read about it?"

"Yeah. Last night." He shrugged his shoulders, trying to look nonchalant. "I looked it up in a book."

Emma regarded him speculatively. He wasn't facing her now, he was staring back at the Farmington house.

"So I was right," she said at last. "You *are* as scared as I am."

"Well, I wouldn't say *scared* exactly. I mean, *scared* is such a strong word. *Concerned* is better, I'm *concerned*, but anyway, nothing's gonna happen. Like I just told you, there's a very logical explanation for that dream you had and—"

"It was more than a dream, Charlie. How many times do I have to tell you?"

Emma started walking again, leaving Charlie to follow and mutter behind her.

"You look like Emma Farmington, you even have

the same first name, and it's been almost a hundred years since the fire," he went on. "That's a centennial—a major milestone, right?" When Emma didn't answer, Charlie rushed on, gaining momentum now from his own genius.

"But another hundred years from now—or—or maybe not even that long—some other girl named Emma could move here, or some guy who happens to be named Daniel, or some mean father with a daughter, and the same thing would happen to them."

But Emma was lost in her own train of thought. "I keep going over it all, you know? Am I supposed to *do* something? *Find* something? *Stop* something?"

"What's done is done," Charlie stated firmly. "You can't go back and change the past . . . you can't go back and rewrite history. And if it's just a matter of exposing Josiah for the murderer he was, nobody'd care about that now anyway."

"I just feel so sad for Daniel and Emma. I mean, their love was so . . . so deep and romantic and real. I've never known two people in love like that." *The way he touched me . . . his kisses . . . the way we fit together . . .* A smile brushed her lips, and her voice grew soft. "I've never been loved like that before now. Before now, I couldn't even imagine how it'd feel."

"Before now?" Charlie snorted. "But now you can?"

Emma froze in her tracks. A rush of color flooded her cheeks, not just from embarrassment but from the shock of unexpected desire.

"Hey, are you okay?"

Charlie's words snapped her back to reality. He was leaning down over her shoulder, trying to peer into her face, and Emma quickly lowered her head.

"Of course I'm okay. Why shouldn't I be okay?"

"What's the matter with you? What are you star-ing at?"

"Nothing."

"What's wrong with your face? You look like a lobster."

"Oh, leave me alone." Shaking him off, Emma hur-ried toward the fence. She could hear him shouting after her, but she pretended not to notice.

"Now what'd I do?" Charlie called. "What are you so mad about?"

Emma began to run. She could hear Charlie yelling, and she could hear Daniel pleading—*"Emma . . . come back to me"*—and her head felt as if it were going to explode. She wanted to turn right around and go back to the Farmington house, back to Daniel and his love and protection—and at the same time she wanted to go home, to her own room, away from Charlie and the whole world and all the doubts and questions spinning ruthlessly through her mind. She didn't understand what was happening to her—*why* it was happening to her—but it had opened up a whole new world of feel-ings and sensations that left her open and aching and vulnerable.

She heard the swift approach of Charlie's foot-steps, and he caught her by the arm just before she reached the fence.

"Wait," he said quietly. "Emma, wait."

She didn't want to talk to him. She didn't want to talk to anyone, but very gently Charlie turned her around.

"What happens to you?" he asked her now, and there was no mockery in his tone, no amusement in his eyes. "What do you do when you're with Daniel?"

Emma met his gaze, all too aware of the blush creeping back into her cheeks. Charlie wasn't laughing at her, and he wasn't angry. For one rare moment Emma saw true compassion on her twin's face.

"Don't you know?" she whispered.

Charlie averted his eyes. She saw him nod. Then he steadily met her gaze once more.

"All I know," he said softly, "is that sometimes I feel how happy you are."

Silence settled between them. This time it was Emma who looked away. The world blurred for an instant through her tears, and she hurriedly wiped them with the back of her hand.

"Look, I don't understand any of this." Charlie sighed. "But what if I went back and spent the night in the cellar. Just to see what happens."

Surprised, Emma stepped back. She blinked away a fresh surge of tears and managed a weak laugh.

"Charlie, you're as crazy as I am." Throwing her arms around him, she squeezed him tightly, feeling the brief touch of his hand upon her head. He tolerated her hug for exactly half a minute before wriggling free.

"Okay, okay," he muttered. "Get off me."

The sleeping bag and backpack had fallen to the ground. As Charlie bent to retrieve them, Emma walked off several paces and spread her arms wide.

"Look, Charlie, I appreciate what you're trying to do. But where do we start? What are we even looking for?"

Her brother cast her a sidelong glance. "You tell me. You're the only one Daniel seems to be interested in." Before Emma could comment, he added, "So let's just say, what if I really did believe you. Let's just say, what if I went along with everything you've told me. Let's just say that some hundred-year-old ghost shows up one day, completely out of the blue, and starts . . . well . . . haunting you."

"Okay," Emma agreed.

"So why's he here? Something must have happened to make him show up."

"You mean besides the fact that I look just like his girlfriend, that she and I are the same age and have the same name, and that I ended up in the cellar where Daniel rescued her?"

Charlie shook his head. "Something's missing. There's no . . . motive."

"Motive?"

"Well, ghosts don't just come back to be sociable, do they? I mean, don't they usually come back 'cause they *want* something?"

Emma considered this. "Or they're emotionally tied to something. Or someone. Or they don't realize they're dead."

"But if that were true, wouldn't he have been hanging around long before now? We've lived here for four years. So why'd he choose this particular weekend for a surprise visit?"

"Because it's almost the hundred year anniversary of our—*their*—death."

Charlie didn't reply. He tossed Emma's things over the fence, hesitated, then leaned forward, curling both hands around the tall iron spikes. His eyes grew pensive as he shot her a narrow glance.

"Or maybe we're overlooking the obvious," he said.

"What do you mean?"

"You said that you—Emma—was still alive when the fire was closing in."

Emma nodded silently. Charlie's expression grew more solemn.

"But Daniel had that stab wound; he'd lost a lot of blood. He was practically dead already when Emma found him."

Again Emma nodded.

"The heat from that fire would've been incredible. With all that wood and hay, the barn would've gone up in a matter of minutes. Nobody could have survived a fire like that. At least . . . that's what everyone would think."

Emma's eyes began to widen. "Then you're saying—"

"I'm saying, what if Emma got out alive?"

19

Emma felt a dizzying rush of emotion.

As she stared at Charlie, the enormity of that long-ago tragedy seemed to hit her full force, an impact that was nearly crushing.

"But how could that be?" she whispered. "I was there. I *saw* it happen."

"You said you saw the fire coming *closer,*" Charlie reminded her. "You never said you actually saw yourself die."

This was true, Emma realized. She shut her eyes against the powerful memory of smoke and flames and the motionless body of Daniel beneath her.

"But if I *did* get out," she said slowly, "then how'd it happen? And where would I have gone?"

Charlie shrugged. "You said it was nighttime. And Josiah was drunk. He probably ran like hell after the fire started, and anyway, he wouldn't have been expecting anyone to escape."

"I don't know, Charlie." Emma opened her eyes once more and slowly shook her head. "This house was out in the middle of nowhere. There wouldn't have been any place to hide, and Emma *must* have hidden. I can't imagine her going back home after her own father tried to kill her. And besides that, Josiah had everyone out looking for her. Somebody would've found her if she'd still been alive."

"Maybe she and Daniel had a secret place," Charlie suggested. "Some special meeting place nobody knew about but them. Maybe Emma went there for a while, then managed to sneak out of town somehow."

The two of them grew silent. Glancing back over his shoulder, Charlie raised his eyes to the upstairs windows of the Farmington house, and Emma sadly followed his gaze.

"If only that house could talk to us, Charlie—tell us its deep, dark secrets. Or maybe if we could find where the barn used to be. Maybe there's still some clue left behind that nobody ever discovered."

"Not very likely after all this time." Charlie started to hoist himself up onto the fence, but Emma pulled him back down.

"Are you sure?" she persisted. "Are you positive there wouldn't be anything?" She made a gesture toward the front yard. "Maybe we could just look around. Just to satisfy our curiosity."

"You're not gonna find any part of that barn, Em. Not when it burned down a hundred years ago."

"How can you be so sure?" Ignoring his logic,

Emma started walking between the two houses, heading for the locked gate and the quiet street beyond. "So where would it've been, exactly? Past our house and down the block somewhere, right?"

"Wrong." Charlie let out a snort, half amused, half disgusted. "Your sense of direction ranks right up there with your social life. Don't you remember the pictures?"

Emma bristled. "Yes. And the barn was way out in front of the house, closer to the road and—"

"I know, I know, and that's what's been bothering me," Charlie cut her off. "I kept thinking about those photos, how something didn't seem quite right. So this morning I really looked at them again. In the book you copied from, the barn was on the southeast side of the house. But in the *newspaper*, you can see the piles of ashes and where the grass is all burnt away—on the *northeast* side of the house."

Emma looked confused "Wait a minute—"

"Which means the picture in the book must've been taken sometime *after* the fire," Charlie explained. "Which means he must've rebuilt the barn on a different spot."

"Why not build it back where it was to begin with?"

"Would *you* want people working around the place where you murdered somebody? Wondering if evidence might show up?"

Without waiting for her to comment, Charlie scaled the fence and pointed to the jagged line of unkempt lawns angling away down the street.

"So you're right about part of it. The barnyard would've been off around there somewhere—but the *second* barnyard, not the first one. The barn itself was probably bigger than our house—the Farmington property would've taken up this whole neighborhood."

Emma had joined him now, hanging on to the fence to get a better view. "So the original barn was—where? The houses running behind us? But at the other end of our street?"

"Probably around where the Miss Lobergs live. They're at the very edge of what's left of the neighborhood, and they're on a huge lot, almost as big as the Farmington place is now."

Emma shuddered in spite of herself. "Great. So we're gonna march up to their door and ask if we can explore their garden?"

"Are you insane?" Charlie climbed over, landing lightly on the other side. "You can't go around harassing the neighbors. What are you gonna say to them, anyway—'Oh, hello there, I'm looking for a guy who was murdered here about a hundred years ago'?"

"I thought you wanted to help me."

"I do wanna help you, but—"

"I knew it was too good to last," Emma grumbled. "What was I thinking? That just because you were actually nice to me for one whole second—"

"Knock it off, Em." Reaching up, Charlie tugged her over the fence, then gathered her things once more. "Look, I *do* wanna help you. I *will* help you. But—"

Abruptly he broke off. Emma saw his gaze fix upon her left hand, and she quickly tried to slip it behind her back.

"You're still wearing that ring," Charlie said.

Emma shook her head. She gave the ring a nervous

twist and looked the other way.

"I told you to throw it back down in the cellar," Charlie went on, his tone growing angry. "No, on second thought *I'll* throw it—I don't want you going anywhere near that house again." He paused, his frown deepening. "Jeez, Em, maybe it's just that simple. Maybe if you got rid of that stupid ring, Daniel'd go back to wherever he came from."

Emma didn't answer. Again she twisted the tiny gold band, and a stab of panic went through her. *Get rid of the ring?* Images of Daniel flooded her mind, and her heart beat faster. *What if Charlie's right? What if I give back the ring and never see Daniel again?*

"That *is* what you want," Charlie reminded her.

Emma's head snapped up. She stared full into Charlie's eyes.

"Em," he repeated slowly. "That *is* what you want. Right?"

Guiltily she managed a nod. "Sure. Of course it is."

"Then give it to me."

A second stab, much worse this time, despair and utter desperation aching through her. Her thoughts were one dark jumble, clouding her mind, confusing her as Charlie held out his hand.

"Emma, *give* it to me."

Unconsciously she took a step back. She saw the surprise on Charlie's face, and then the concern, and she tightened her left hand into a fist.

"You said you felt how happy I was," she insisted, almost pleadingly.

"Come on, Em, what's the matter with you? Don't act stupid."

As Charlie made a sudden grab for her arm, Emma swerved out of his reach. She stumbled and nearly fell, then caught herself again, still putting distance between them.

"I can't give it back yet, Charlie. I can't. Daniel *wanted* me to have it, don't you see?"

"See what?" Charlie demanded. "Where do you think you're going?"

But Emma didn't answer. She turned and she ran, and she didn't stop running until she was halfway up the street.

20

She didn't have a clue what she was doing.

She didn't know why she'd suddenly panicked, why she'd felt so threatened and lashed out at Charlie the way she had. He'd only been trying to help her. He'd only been trying to . . .

"Save me," Emma whispered.

She stopped in her tracks and looked around her.

Had that been *her* voice speaking aloud just then? Or had it been the voice of *another* Emma, a voice silenced for nearly a hundred years?

A deep, cold shiver worked its way up Emma's spine.

She thrust both hands into the pockets of her jacket and continued along the sidewalk.

She knew Charlie was right—she knew there'd be nothing left of the original barn after so long a time. In fact, she didn't know why she was even still walking toward the Loberg house at all. She had absolutely no desire to run into those crazy old women, and being near the actual site of the murder would only make her more depressed than she was already.

Yet Emma kept walking. She ducked her head and followed the crumbling pavement and tried to not think about Daniel.

It seemed a long way to where the sisters lived. Again Emma was struck by the shabbiness of the neighborhood, the boarded-up houses, litter-filled yards, the overwhelming air of desolation. For the millionth time she wished she could move away from here, have a modern house with fresh paint and solid floors, and friendly neighbors who always smiled and waved, and a great big shopping mall close by.

Her bad mood grew even worse. By the time she reached the other end of the neighborhood, she was cold and tired and ready to go back. She crossed the street, then stopped to catch her breath. She wished Charlie would come looking for her and drive her home. She wished she'd never heard of the Farmington place, never seen Daniel, never stepped foot outside her nice, safe bedroom door. And all the while she was wishing, she was staring over at the house where the Loberg sisters lived.

It was almost as spooky as the Farmington place. Almost as big, too, but surrounded by a lot more trees. In fact, the house itself was nearly invisible beneath gnarled, twisted oaks and elms and brown cascades of brittle ivy, behind trellises and birdhouses and painted statuary and a solid row of windchimes that ran the entire length of the porch.

Emma shook her head in wonder. Apparently the sisters hadn't killed off any strays for quite some time—the porch and front steps and brick pathway were crawling with dozens of cats—very well-fed, by the looks of them—and almost as many kittens, tumbling about in the dead grass. As Emma's gaze swept over the scene, she also noted the huge fenced lot off to one side, complete with potting shed, an apple orchard, and the biggest vegetable garden she'd ever seen.

Okay, you've come this far. What now?

Suddenly Emma felt foolish. She didn't know what she'd expected to find here—or *feel* here, for that matter. Some remnant of ghostly past that would tie up neatly to the present? She focused her attention on the yard, remembering what Charlie had said. *The original barn would've stood right about there, maybe. . . . It would've been just after dark. . . . The two young lovers would've been running for their lives. . . .*

Emma closed her eyes and took a deep breath. *Help me, Daniel. You dragged me into this. . . . What do you want me to do?*

Before she even realized it, she'd scrambled over the chicken wire and was walking toward the garden. All the produce had been harvested by this time, but there was still a tired-looking scarecrow keeping watch in the center. Emma crept past it, feeling strangely unnerved. Its head was drooping low on its chest, yet she had the distinct feeling it was watching her.

Again she stopped. She glanced back over her shoulder, but the street was deserted. There were no sounds from the house, nothing silhouetted in any of the windows.

Her skin began to crawl. For just an instant she thought she smelled smoke . . . heard the faraway echo of screams. . . .

"Emma! Stay with me!"

"I *am* with you, Daniel!" Emma's voice rose above the phantom death cries, and she choked on the acrid fumes. "I'm right *here!*"

"He's in torment," the voice said behind her.

Emma screamed and whirled around.

The small figure who stood there was wearing a purple jumper and workboots, and her long silver hair frizzed out around her head.

"He's not a dream," Emma said, almost pleadingly. "Daniel's real!"

"Of course Daniel's real," a Miss Loberg said calmly. "And you must be Emma."

21

〜∞〜

This particular Miss Loberg was old and wrinkled and stood less than five feet tall. She reminded Emma of a small, bright bird—not someone even remotely capable of eating little children or preying upon strays.

"How do you know my name?" Emma demanded.

"Oh, we know everything that goes on in the neighborhood. Not that there's ever much going on anymore. Not that there's much neighborhood left for anything to go on in. But when you and your family moved here, we knew right away."

"You . . . knew *what?*"

"That you were Emma, of course. There's certainly no mistaking the resemblance. And we also knew it was only a matter of time. One whole century tomorrow." Miss Loberg paused, then sadly shook her head.

"Poor Daniel. One can hardly listen to his anguish and not be deeply touched by it."

Emma continued to stare.

"Naturally, we would have done something for him long before now," Miss Loberg went on, "but it would have been quite impossible. Quite impossible without you, my dear. You're the key to the whole solution."

"What . . . how . . . you *know* about Daniel?" As the woman regarded her curiously, Emma gestured in the direction of the garden.

"Of course," Miss Loberg replied. "Won't you come in?" Then, when Emma hesitated, she added, "I assure you, there are no little children on the menu today."

Emma nodded sheepishly. The smaller Miss Loberg smiled.

"This way," she said, leading Emma inside.

The house wasn't at all what Emma had expected. Cluttered and cozy, overflowing with plants and framed photographs, china teacups and bric-a-brac, chintz-covered furniture and the smell of fresh-baked bread, the house seemed to wrap welcoming arms around her. She quickly found herself in a front parlor, seated on a velvet loveseat, with a cup of hot tea and a plateful of cookies in her hand. As she tried to make space on the coffee table for her saucer, Miss Loberg hurried over to a curtained doorway and called loudly.

"Sister! We have company!"

"Who's that?" a prim voice snapped back.

"It's *Emma*, dear!" Miss Loberg answered. "*Emma!*"

The curtain opened at once. Emma recognized the other, taller Miss Loberg, who stood for a moment scrutinizing their guest with narrowed eyes, her elegant hands deftly repinning barrettes into her snowy-white hair.

"Well, you certainly took your time coming here," the taller Miss Loberg said irritably. She seated herself in a dainty chair opposite the loveseat and proceeded to watch Emma like an imperious hawk.

"So." The shorter Miss Loberg smiled. "I see you're wearing the ring."

Emma held up her hand in surprise. "How do you know about the ring?"

"She's wearing the ring, Sister!" The shorter Miss Loberg seemed delighted. "The one Daniel told Betsey about, that he bought for Emma—the one with the sweet little heart! Isn't that lovely? Everything is unfolding exactly as it should."

"I see it," the older one snapped. "I'm not blind, you know."

Emma shut her eyes. Tried to collect her thoughts. Opened her eyes again.

"I . . . don't understand any of this," she confessed. "I'm not even sure why I came here today. It's just that—"

"You came here to help Daniel," the shorter Miss Loberg told her patiently. "Because you're the only one who can."

Again Emma paused . . . shut her eyes . . . opened them once more.

"Look—" she began, but tall Miss Loberg cut her off.

"Just get on with it, girl. Do you want him to suffer another hundred years?"

"Well . . ." Emma looked helplessly from one to the other. "Well, I don't—"

"God knows *I* don't want him suffering another

hundred years!" tall Miss Loberg exploded. "All that ghostly business going on out there in the garden—it's enough to drive a teetotaler to drink!"

The short Miss Loberg leaned toward Emma with a conspiratorial whisper. "She *does* drink. She has a nip every night in bed."

"Wait." Abruptly Emma stood up. She felt a sudden urge to laugh and cry at the same time but managed to keep her voice even. "Look, will someone please tell me what's happening? I just want to get on with my life—I just want to be normal like everyone else—"

"Oh, sit down," tall Miss Loberg said. "Quit being so dramatic."

"Well, she really *doesn't* understand, Sister," short Miss Loberg fretted. Very gently she pushed Emma back down onto the loveseat. "Perhaps we'd better start at the beginning."

Emma put one hand to her forehead. *Maybe I'm having another weird vision. Maybe I'm not really here at all. Maybe I'm home taking a nap, and all of this is just some sort of nightmare, and what sort of insanity have I dreamt up this time?*

"According to the legend," short Miss Loberg began, but Emma interrupted.

"Excuse me, but what legend?"

"Our family legend. Well, I suppose one could call it a legend," the woman mused. "Or perhaps it's only gossip or hearsay. Nevertheless, it's the story that was passed down to us by our grandmother."

"I wouldn't exactly say 'passed down,'" tall Miss Loberg sniffed. "It wasn't as if this was ever mentioned in respectable company, you know."

Short Miss Loberg rolled her eyes. "There was a scandal. Many years ago, when one of our cousins worked as a cook in the Farmington household."

Emma's eyes widened. "Betsey?"

"Yes. Betsey. Josiah Farmington was a mean, stingy man—the richest man in the whole county, and by far the most cruel. He had a beautiful daughter, kind and generous, everyone said so—"

"Everyone *who*?" her sister demanded. "Just stick to the facts."

Short Miss Loberg heaved an annoyed sigh. "At any rate, she fell in love with the stableboy. Daniel Frye. Oh, my, but he was a handsome young man! But Josiah was insanely possessive of Emma—he completely controlled her in every way. And she did what he demanded—she wouldn't have dared otherwise! Why, Betsey was witness to some *very* severe beatings when Emma tried to defy him. In fact, more than once Betsey sneaked food to poor Emma when Josiah locked her away for days at a time with nothing to eat."

"I knew that," Emma mumbled to herself, but no one seemed to be listening.

"Poor Daniel nearly went mad, he worried so about her."

"Josiah was the mad one," tall Miss Loberg snapped. "Get on with it."

As short Miss Loberg defiantly squared her shoulders, Emma hid a smile.

"One evening Daniel and Emma tried to escape once and for all. Josiah was supposed to be away, tending to matters of business, and it was Betsey's day off—

she'd walked over to a neighboring farm where her friend looked after the farmer's young children. So Daniel and Emma should have been able to leave without any problems. But then . . . oh, dear . . . things didn't work out quite the way they expected. . . ."

While short Miss Loberg drew an unsteady breath, Emma steeled herself against a fresh onslaught of memories. And once again, as with the times before, she heard the screams, the roar of flames, she felt the panic and hopelessness of impending death. . . .

"No one ever really knew what happened," short Miss Loberg said. "There was a terrible fire, and by the time it was over, there was nothing left but ashes. Betsey said she could see the smoke and flames a mile away as she came across the fields, and by the time she reached the barn, Josiah was already there, just arrived home. She said he was in a rage, screaming that his daughter had been kidnapped, that his money had been stolen, that Daniel had taken everything that belonged to him. He was like a madman, Betsey said, cursing Daniel's name and swearing he would never rest until Daniel Frye was dead."

Silence hung heavy in the room. Lace curtains ruffled at a half-open window, and Emma pressed both hands to her face.

"Josiah didn't go off on a trip that day," she mumbled. "He never even left the house. He was drunk, and he caught Daniel and Emma when they were trying to leave."

"Yes, that was what Betsey always suspected." Short Miss Loberg picked up her own dainty cup and took several small sips. She stirred her tea with her spoon, and her voice was sorrowful. "Betsey always believed there had been foul play of some kind. But of course she could never prove anything. And Daniel and Emma were never seen again."

Emma's hands lowered to her lap. She swallowed a lump in her throat. "They didn't get away that night, Miss Loberg. They were both in the barn when it burned down."

"Yes," she replied softly. "Just as Betsey thought."

"But it was even worse than that. Josiah murdered Daniel with a pitchfork. That's how the fire started, when a lantern fell over, and Josiah shut them inside and just left them there."

"Monster!" tall Miss Loberg snorted. "That Josiah Farmington was a monster of the worst kind! *He's* the one who should have been trussed up and roasted!"

Short Miss Loberg nodded in agreement. "Apparently that's what *most* people wished back then. Many of them never believed Josiah's story anyway, you know—about Daniel stealing the family silver and taking Emma against her will. But Josiah was a very powerful man, and people were afraid to cross him."

"As Betsey always said," her sister echoed.

"You see, my dear, Sister and I know what we know because of family stories, because of Betsey." Short Miss Loberg leaned toward Emma, her voice gently matter-of-fact. "So now you must tell us. How do you know what *you* know?"

Emma stared back at her for a long moment. She shifted her gaze reluctantly to the other sister. Neither Miss Loberg uttered a word. They simply sat there and fixed Emma with polite expressions and formal smiles.

"Well, dear?" short Miss Loberg urged. "If you're worried about us being skeptical, you needn't be."

At last Emma nodded. Then, after several fumbling starts, she told them the whole story.

About how she'd come to be at the Farmington house that night, how she'd fallen through the porch, and then the whole vivid episode which had followed. She was surprised at herself for being so open with these two women she barely knew, but somehow it felt easy, almost comforting, to confide in them. She even told how she'd gone back to the house the second time and ended up in Emma's old bedroom, but left out the intimate details between Daniel and Emma.

"Emma wanted to die," she finished. "She *prayed* to die before the flames could get to her. And she didn't want to live without Daniel."

"Bless them." Short Miss Loberg pulled a handkerchief from the pocket of her jumper and dabbed at the corners of her eyes. "Poor Emma. Poor, sweet Daniel."

"Oh, stop going on about it," tall Miss Loberg scowled. "One tortured soul around here is quite enough. Just tell her the rest of it."

Emma watched curiously as short Miss Loberg leaned over and gently patted her hand.

"With all due respect, my dear," the woman began politely, "we believe your story, but we don't really believe that Emma died in that fire."

"You . . . you don't?"

"Not a chance!" Tall Miss Loberg looked at Emma as if she were a total imbecile. "And this ring you're wearing confirms it! How *else* could it possibly have survived?"

"And why else would poor Daniel keep calling for his Emma?" short Miss Loberg whispered. "The misery is almost more than one can bear."

"Betsey *always* had a suspicion," the other Miss Loberg said yet again.

"Yes, that's true," her sister replied. "Betsey always had a feeling that *somehow* Emma managed to escape. Managed to get away and build a new life for herself, where her father could never find her." Short Miss Loberg pondered a moment, then added, "At least, that's what Betsey *hoped*."

"So Charlie was right," Emma mumbled, and now both sisters bent forward in their chairs. "My brother," Emma explained. "My brother Charlie—".

"Oh, we know who your brother is," tall Miss Loberg interrupted, her cheeks flushing suddenly pink.

"We think he's quite . . . how would you say it?—a stud," her sister confided.

Emma sat back incredulously. She cleared her throat and struggled to hold back a laugh. "Well," she managed at last, "I'll tell him you said so."

"Oh, no, please don't," short Miss Loberg insisted. "We'd be absolutely mortified, wouldn't we, Sister?"

"Just tell us about his theory," tall Miss Loberg demanded, and once more Emma hid a smile.

"Exactly what you were saying. That maybe somehow Emma got out of the barn at the last minute, and that's why Daniel's come back looking for her."

The two sisters looked very pleased with themselves.

"If Emma got out, then you must remember it." Almost accusingly tall Miss Loberg narrowed her eyes, pinning Emma to the seat cushions. "You must remember how it happened."

Emma's mind immediately spun back as she tried to recall the horrific scene in the barn.

"I . . . I didn't," she insisted. "I didn't escape. That's what I remember."

"But you *must* have escaped. Think, girl. You must have found a way out at the last possible second, and you're just blocking it out."

"No, Emma was dying. There was fire all around."

Emma's voice rose anxiously. She didn't want to think about it—it hurt to go back, it was too horrible to remember. For a brief second she tried to concentrate, then held back a moan. It was too frightening—too *real*!

A crash . . . there was a crash . . .

"I—*she*—tried to shield Daniel from the flames, and she was praying to die, and then . . ."

A crash, very close by . . . a deafening crash, a blistering surge of heat billowing over me, suffocating waves, sparks flying, embers falling . . .

"This is much too painful for her, Sister," short Miss Loberg scolded. "Leave it for now."

Tall Miss Loberg's spine stiffened against the back of her chair. "Hmmph. She was there, for pity's sake, she ought to remember."

But Emma looked back at her weakly. Beyond the crashing sound and the overpowering sense of loss there was only darkness.

"So what if Emma Farmington really did live, and Daniel died," she concluded softly. "That still doesn't explain why I'm involved in this thing."

"Because it *has* to be you, dear," the shorter Miss

Loberg explained patiently. "You've been separated for much too long. He misses you, and he wants to be with you again. Don't you see?"

Emma shook her head. She didn't see at all.

"You're his Emma," her hostess went on. "*Daniel's* Emma. And you've obviously traveled here again, all the way from your human existence nearly a century ago. To save Daniel from eternal misery."

"Wait." Emma was frowning even harder now, setting her cup in its saucer, standing on wobbly knees. "Wait a minute. You're saying—*what* are you saying?"

"Reincarnation, dear. Past lives. Don't tell me you've never considered the possibility—"

"Destiny," tall Miss Loberg snapped. "There's no use even thinking about it, it's already preordained. You'll just have to be brave."

"*What's* preordained?" Emma asked. She was more than confused now—she could feel little needles of fear racing up and down her spine. "I don't understand—"

"This time, when it happens—" short Miss Loberg began, but Emma burst out at them.

"*This time!* When *what* happens? What are you talking about?"

"*This* time," tall Miss Loberg snapped. "Are you deaf?"

Short Miss Loberg stood up. She reached across the coffee table and took Emma gently by the shoulders. She looked deep into the girl's frightened eyes.

"I'm so sorry, dear." Her voice was soft and kind. "But this time I expect you'll have to *join* Daniel. This time I expect you'll have to die."

22

Emma had a weird sensation of being out of body.

For a long, long while she simply stood there like a distant observer, watching her other self trapped between the coffee table and the loveseat, while two old ladies chatted anxiously back and forth, and one of them tried to push her back into a sitting position. She thought she heard herself say something, mutter some rude remark, and she knew she wanted to bolt for the door, but her feet seemed rooted to the finely polished floorboards.

She finally began to come back to herself when she felt cold water on her face.

"Well," tall Miss Loberg sniffed, "*that* was certainly tactful of you, Sister!"

"Oh, my dear, I do apologize!" the other Miss Loberg fretted, taking another pass at Emma's face with the washcloth. "I didn't dream you'd take it so hard! And I do *so* wish we could have known you longer!"

But by this time Emma felt recovered enough to push the washcloth away. She stood up and made her way determinedly around the furniture and to the front door, while both the sisters watched.

"I'm going now," Emma declared. "Thank you for the tea."

Neither one said anything; neither one tried to stop her. She slammed the door behind her, stopped, flung it open again, and glared in at them.

"What would make you say something like that?" Emma railed. "Are you crazy?"

The sisters exchanged cautious glances. Then, very slowly, short Miss Loberg crossed to a table in the corner, opened a small wooden box, and withdrew a yellowed sheet of folded paper.

Without another word she approached Emma. She held the paper out to her and stood by silently as Emma took it reluctantly from her hand.

The paper was brittle with age. The writing was faded, a dull, dark, reddish-brown color—and scratchy and uneven, as though written by a frail, palsied hand.

I am glad to die.
Life has held no meaning without you, my love.
And so I make my last earthly wish. That someday, in some kinder, gentler world, God will grant us the opportunity to change what could not be changed in this lifetime. And then, we shall be together.
Forever.

Emma's chest felt painfully tight.
As though her heart were breaking.

"This was found among Betsey's things after she died," short Miss Loberg said. "The wooden box originally belonged to Emma Farmington, given to her by Betsey when Emma was a child. It was one of Emma's most precious possessions. Since the box went missing when Emma disappeared, Betsey assumed that Emma had taken the box with her when she and Daniel tried to escape, and that it had ultimately been lost in the fire. But Grandmother told us that Betsey found the box again, many years after Josiah passed away."

Emma was intent on every word. "Where was it?"

"In a hollow tree where Emma and Daniel used to meet and leave messages for each other. Betsey knew about it, of course—she often sneaked Emma's notes out of the house, and she also acted as lookout, warning them when Josiah was due home."

"So nobody ever saw Emma leaving the box?"

"Oh, goodness no. The house had been through several different owners by that time, and Betsey was far up in years. She'd found employment in another town after Josiah's death, and apparently was in very poor health. Grandmother said she only came back for sentimental reasons, really. Just to see the house one more time and—"

"The box couldn't have been there very long," the tall Miss Loberg broke in, sounding exasperated. "Its condition is quite remarkable. Not the condition of something that's been left out in the elements for any length of time."

"And the writing appears feeble," added her sister. "Grandmother said Betsey never talked about it, but Grandmother's favorite theory was that Emma, old and dying, had returned one last time to the only place she'd ever been truly happy. And she hid the box there, her final message to Daniel."

Emma didn't know what to say. Very slowly she refolded the paper and handed it back to the smaller Miss Loberg.

"So you see?" short Miss Loberg added reasonably. "The minute you moved into the neighborhood, Sister and I *knew*. The minute we saw your face and learned your name, we *knew* you were the one. That destiny was unfolding in proper order."

"Wait." Emma heard herself beginning to babble. "Just because I happen to have Emma's name—I mean, coincidences happen all the time—"

"This is no coincidence," tall Miss Loberg snapped. "That message was written on the very threshold of death. In Emma Farmington's own blood."

Emma's eyes widened. "That's insane! You don't know that! You're just coming up with all these different theories, putting all these meanings into them, and you can't really know—"

"Accept it." Tall Miss Loberg rose from her chair. She seemed to rise right into the ceiling. "Look at the color, child. Of course it's blood. And whatever is sworn in blood, in the face of death, is a *covenant*. A truth made with God."

"I'm afraid my sister is right," short Miss Loberg whispered with the faintest trace of a smile. "All the signs seem to point that way. No doubt it *will* happen again, just as it did before. Only this time the outcome will be different. This time the both of you will be truly happy."

Emma turned and stumbled from the room. She

had the vague sensation of windchimes crashing, loud discordant notes in her head, and tripping over cats and little stone elves as she raced for the front gate. She didn't stop running till she saw her own house directly ahead of her, and even then she burst through the door and fumbled frantically to lock it behind her.

She wasn't sure how long she leaned there against the door, gasping for breath. She felt dizzy and light-headed; her brain was pounding so violently, she felt as if it might explode at any second. *Crazy!* She'd heard the rumors about the Miss Lobergs, but she'd down-played most of them to mere age and eccentricity. And now to discover how right everyone had been, how totally insane those two sisters really were—

"*This time . . . you'll have to die.*"

"Charlie!" she tried to call but managed only a groan.

She couldn't hear any noise from upstairs. She figured Charlie must have gone out with his stupid friends, and Mom would be sleeping now.

Why'd I ever go there? Why'd I ever go to that crazy house, anyway? I knew there wouldn't be anything left to see, I knew there wouldn't be anything left to find—

She pressed both hands to her head, but her thoughts spun in all directions. She could still remember how calm and polite her reception had been, how utterly expected. *They were* waiting *for me,* Emma thought miserably. *They were waiting for me to show up at their house, they knew I'd come, everything's happened just the way they believed it would.*

"They're insane," Emma mumbled, and then she frowned. *If you really believe those sisters are insane, then why are you getting so upset?*

Mulling this over, she forced herself to sit down on the couch. For that matter, the Miss Lobergs could have been making everything up, she told herself. There was no real proof the box had ever been with Betsey's things, that it had ever even *belonged* to Emma Farmington. No proof the letter was genuine or that the dull-colored ink had anything to do with the blood of a grieving woman. Old people lived in worlds of their own, Emma reminded herself firmly. They invented fantasies and scenarios from lifetimes of joys and sorrows and dreams and disappointments—and who could really know for sure what was real or just a figment of worn-out imaginations?

For a brief second Emma almost felt sorry for them. Two lonely women living out dramas in their otherwise empty existence . . .

But those details . . . They knew all those details. . . .

"Anyone can take a dumb old legend and embellish it," Emma whispered. She leaned her head back against the cushions and closed her eyes, still talking to herself. "They could make up anything, anything at all! There's no one alive today to argue the facts, and nobody'll ever know for sure exactly what happened."

She squeezed back a sting of tears. *But they said they could hear Daniel out in their garden, they talked about how unhappy he sounds.*

"No, it's stupid. It's all ridiculous, and I won't listen."

And that is where the original barn once stood, that is where all the bad stuff happened, Charlie said so. . . .

She wished Charlie were here right now. Even though it was late morning, the sun had disappeared behind metal gray clouds, and the sky was threatening snow. Little cyclones of dead leaves spun across the yard. A dark chill seemed to envelop the house.

Emma glanced anxiously into the hall. She was being foolish, she knew, but the sisters' prophecy continued to haunt her, and no matter how she tried to rationalize or dismiss what had happened, it only loomed larger in her mind.

The house was unnervingly quiet. As she hurried up to her room, she thought about waking her mother, then decided against it. *What could I tell her, anyway? I wouldn't even know where to start.* She jumped into bed and pulled her legs tightly to her chest, resting her chin on her knees. She told herself how silly she was being, how glad she was now that Charlie *wasn't* here, knowing how much he'd make fun of her. She told herself she was safe, yet at the same time she felt herself getting up and walking to her window.

She didn't want to look.

She didn't want to look over at the house next door, but she couldn't seem to help herself.

Because something *wanted* her to look.

Suddenly Emma could feel it, in the very pit of her soul—*just like I felt it that very first night, the eerie presence, those invisible eyes watching from the second-story window, forcing me to look,* needing *me to look . . .*

"What do you *want* with me?" She slammed her palms flat against the windowpane, and her voice sounded like a stranger's voice, someone she didn't even recognize. "Tell me what happened that night! Tell me what to do!"

She could see that upstairs window even now; she was positive the lace curtains moved there ever so slightly, that a pale shadow beckoned her from the darkness beyond. . . .

"How can I help you?" Emma cried. "Don't you understand? I'm getting so scared, and we're running out of time!"

She hit the window again, the glass rattling dangerously beneath her fingers, and all her emotions were crumbling, she could feel herself falling apart. *I can't get away from him, even here, even now—oh, God, it's not true, please, please don't let me die!*

"No!" And again she hit the windowpane, again and again, and she could hear someone screaming, *"No, no!"* but it was as if the sound drifted to her from some other place, from some other person in some other time . . . *"No . . . no!"*

"Emma?"

The familiar voice came out of nowhere, an unwelcome intrusion into her brain. It brought her back with a shock, and as Emma spun around, she saw Val and Charlie standing just inside her bedroom door. Both of them were staring at her as if she were a total lunatic.

Emma held their gaze for one endless moment.

Then her anger exploded.

"What are you doing in here?" She was furious and confused and terrified. She reached out for her dressing table to steady herself, and her voice rose, trembling with rage. "What are you looking at?"

"What are *you* looking at?" Charlie accused her. "Or better yet, who are you talking to?"

Emma stubbornly shook her head. "Nobody. Nothing. Myself."

Before Charlie could answer, a door opened down

the hall and their mother's voice called out sleepily. "Emma? What's wrong?"

Emma saw the quick expression on Charlie's face, the one he always got when he knew he had the upper hand. She pleaded at him with her eyes, and after an uncertain pause, Charlie finally glanced back toward the hall.

"TV, Mom," he said grudgingly. "Sorry."

Val looked completely mystified.

"Honey, are you sure?" Mrs. Donovan fretted. "It sounded like Emma."

"She's fine," Charlie assured her. "We'll turn it down. Go back to sleep."

"Well . . . okay, sweetheart. If you're sure."

"I'm sure," Charlie mumbled. He waited for their mother's door to close, then took a menacing step toward his sister. "I'm sure you've gone totally off the deep end!"

"What's—" Val began, but Charlie cut her off.

"It was *him*," he said angrily. "Wasn't it, Em?"

Emma lowered her eyes, trying to sound more confident than she felt. "I don't know what you're talking about."

"*Him*," Charlie insisted. "And you know exactly what I'm talking about."

Val had been glancing first at one twin and then the other, but now her baffled gaze settled on Emma. "Him who?"

"Tell her," Charlie said unexpectedly. He ignored the venomous look his sister shot him and added, "If you don't tell her, I will."

"Him *who*?" Val demanded.

Biting her lip, Emma turned her back on the two of them. Resentment and frustration raged through her; she felt like she was being violated. "You have no right," she muttered.

"I have every right!" Charlie countered without hesitation. "Enough's enough, Em! Did you hear yourself just now? Do you even realize how close you came to busting out that window? This situation's way past serious—I have every right in the world."

Despite her obvious confusion, Val tried to be soothing. "Look, Em, Charlie's just trying to help. When he couldn't find you, he drove over to my house to see if you were—"

"Charlie's *not* trying to help! I don't *need* Charlie's help!"

"Oh, you need help, all right," Charlie replied with maddening calm. "And don't think for one minute I can't tell when you're deliberately tuning me out."

Again Emma whirled to face him. "Then quit trying to get inside my thoughts!"

"Will someone please tell me what's happening?" Val said helplessly. "Have both of you lost your minds?"

Charlie shook his head. "Just one of us."

"I haven't lost my mind," Emma argued. "I can't help it if I'm the one he comes to—I can't help it if you can't see him!"

"Who's *him*?" Val asked for the third time, only now she cast an uneasy glance about the room. "Are we alone in here?"

"You know, I'm not sure anymore!" Charlie's voice dripped with sarcasm. He made a sweeping gesture toward each of the four walls. "But it wouldn't surprise me if he was in the closet. Or . . . I don't know . . . under the covers, maybe."

"That's not funny, Charlie," Emma said tightly.

"No, Em, it's not."

The twins glared at each other, neither one backing down. Val nervously cleared her throat.

"I . . . think maybe I should go. Okay, then? Bye."

She started to leave, but Charlie caught her by the elbow. Val looked up at him in surprise.

"Nobody's going anywhere till Emma does some explaining," Charlie announced. "So go on, Emma. Explain."

There'd be no getting out of this one—Emma could tell by the grim lines of Charlie's face and the steel in his eyes. With a sigh of defeat, she sat down on the edge of her bed.

"His name's Daniel," she said softly. "Daniel Frye. And he . . . he loves me."

Val's eyes widened. She thought for a minute, frowned, then shook her head in bewilderment.

"Do I even know this guy? Does he go to our school?"

"No." Emma gazed calmly back at her. "He's dead."

23

For a long time there was nothing but silence.

Charlie stared at a spot on the ceiling, and Val continued to watch Emma with a startled, almost comical expression. And then, at last, Val laughed.

"He's *dead*?" she echoed. "You're kidding, right?"

Nobody answered. Val tried again.

"So what's the big deal? I mean, that pretty much describes half the guys at school. If you two want to play a joke on me, you can come up with something much better than that."

The silence had grown uncomfortable now. Emma gazed down at the floor. Charlie shifted positions, crossing his arms over his chest. As Val looked from one of them to the other, her smile began to fade.

"You're . . . serious," she said softly.

The twins nodded in unison. Val walked over to the

bed, nudged Emma aside, and sat down next to her.

"You're really serious," she said again. "And I'm starting to feel like I'm in the middle of some weird movie. I mean, you're really not just doing this to play a trick on me, right? I mean, this is for real?"

Again the twins nodded, more soberly this time. Val nodded back, took a deep breath, and slid one arm around Emma's shoulders.

"Well. Okay. I guess you'd better tell me everything, then."

Emma remained quiet. A tangle of raw emotions still throbbed inside her—resentment and anger, fear and sadness and resignation—at the prospect of baring her soul all over again. Opening up to the Loberg sisters had been a disaster, and now, sharing Daniel with one more person seemed like an ultimate betrayal. She looked deep into Val's eyes, and she actually wondered for a second if Val and Charlie might have her committed.

"Charlie," Val said suddenly. "Would you please get out of here?"

Emma glanced up, surprised. A flicker of doubt crossed Charlie's face, and he stubbornly held his ground.

"No way. This thing's too out of control."

"Look, I know you're really worried," Val soothed him, "but I think you should leave us alone. This is girl talk."

Charlie still wasn't convinced. He scowled, started to argue, then seemed to think better of it.

"Okay," he murmured sullenly, backing toward the door. "But you've got to promise you'll tell Val everything, Em. I mean it. *Everything.*"

"And no lurking," Val warned him. "If we catch you out in the hall—"

Charlie's hands lifted in surrender. He backed completely out of the room and shut the door behind him.

The girls waited. After several minutes they heard his footsteps down the stairs and then the slam of the kitchen door.

"Now," Val said firmly. Releasing Emma, she sat back to listen. Then, with a sympathetic smile, she reached across and took Emma's hand in her own. "I'm all ears. And I'm siding with Charlie on this one—you'd better tell me *everything*."

Emma gave a reluctant nod. "Only if you promise *not* to tell Charlie the really juicy details. He knows everything but those." She hesitated, frowning. "At least I hope he doesn't know about those."

"Juicy details?" Val brightened. "I swear."

For the second time that day Emma recited her strange tale, beginning with her visit to the Farmington house. Only this time she shared all of it—not just the dramatic events of a century ago, but how those events were beginning to steadily take over the present. She told Val about the private times she'd shared with Daniel, their intimate moments of passion, the way those passions still lingered long after her dreams had faded. How he was still so alive to her, so powerfully real. How terrified she was of slipping back into the past, yet even more terrified of never seeing Daniel again. How guilty she felt over Charlie's worry and anger, and how much she resented him for it, even though she knew he only meant to protect her. How she'd visited the Lobergs, the things they'd known, the warning they'd given her when she'd left. She told Val everything she could possibly remember, all her words and emotions spilling out, while Val just sat there and listened and held her hand.

"The Miss Lobergs told me I'll have to die this time, Val," Emma finally concluded. "They told me it's gonna happen again, and this time Emma has to die. And then I came home from there, and something just pulled me to my window, like Daniel was over there in the house next door, wanting me to come. And it's like he's getting stronger, and I can feel it, but I don't know what to do." Her voice lowered to a miserable whisper. "I love him, Val. I know this whole thing is crazy, but . . . I love him."

For a long while neither girl said anything. Then Val gave a long sigh, turned loose of Emma's hand, and curled up in one corner of the bed.

"Wow," she said softly. "You've been acting so funny—I knew something must be going on—but I had no idea . . ."

She left the thought unfinished. The two friends looked at each another.

"Why didn't you tell me before, Em?" she finally asked.

It wasn't said unkindly, but Emma could sense the hurt in Val's voice. Guilt went through her, along with a strange sense of relief at having told Val the truth.

"I wish I had," she admitted now. "It was just all so strange. At first the whole thing seemed unreal, like a dream. A one-time accident . . . or mistake . . . or something crazy. But then . . ."

Emma dropped her eyes. She felt her throat fill

with tears, and she swallowed hard, forcing them back down.

"But then I didn't *want* to share it," she said quietly. "Especially not with you."

Val didn't respond. Several moments passed before Emma could go on, and when she did, she sounded deeply ashamed.

"Because it was just about me, you know? I know it was wrong—it was really selfish and immature—but . . ."

Her voice trailed away. Again she drew a steadying breath.

"It's just that you've always been so popular. You can have your pick of any guy in school, and they always want to go out with you. And then, when this whole thing happened with Daniel . . . for the first time *I* had somebody, too. And Daniel and I—I mean, Emma Farmington—were so connected, so completely in love with each other, that I just . . . just . . ."

"You felt special," Val said softly. "And what is there to feel selfish about, anyway?" Her lips moved in a faint smile. "It's *him*, isn't it? Your dream guy. That perfect one you've always been waiting for?"

When Emma said nothing, Val leaned over and put her arms around her. Then she hugged Emma tightly.

"I'm so sorry, Em."

"You shouldn't be sorry—*I'm* the one who should be sorry. And I mean, I *am* sorry." Sniffling, Emma hugged her friend back. "I don't mean to be jealous of you, Val—I don't *want* to be jealous of you—"

"I know, I know, and it's okay. Don't you realize there've been times when I wished I could be just like *you*?"

Startled, Emma pulled away. She stared into Val's eyes and saw her friend's own mixture of guilt and relief. "Like me?" she echoed.

"Of course like you. That I could have your confidence? Your self-esteem?"

"Val, what on earth are you talking about? I don't have—"

"You've never needed a guy to make you feel better about yourself. You can be your own person without a boyfriend, and you've never settled. You've set your standards and held out for what you want, and you don't worry about what other people think. Don't you see," Val added earnestly, "how lucky you are?"

"But I can't really have him. He's not really in *this* world—not in *my* world."

"I'm not just talking about Daniel. I don't think you even realize how many friends you have at school, or how much you mean to me. And you have this great family—a wonderful mom who really cares about you, and a stupid brother who absolutely adores you."

Emma raised an eyebrow. "Charlie doesn't adore me. He puts up with me 'cause I'm his twin, and we have this connection neither of us can help, and we have to live in the same house."

"I'm serious." Val's expression grew even more solemn, and she rested her hands on Emma's shoulders. "You have so much . . . so much more than me . . . even though it might seem like I have it all."

Emma regarded her silently. After a long while she said, "Okay, maybe I'm good at being on my own, but that doesn't mean I don't get lonely sometimes. I mean, I don't curl up and die 'cause I don't have dates, but I still wish someone would ask me out. I still wish I could be special to just *one* guy. And when Daniel came into my life, I finally knew how it felt to *belong* to somebody. And he was all mine, and that felt so good—"

"It does feel good when it's sincere." Val paused and rolled her eyes. "Unfortunately, I think a lot of guys just ask me out because I live in Posh Park—they don't even care about who I really am."

"Oh, Val," Emma said sadly. "I don't think that's true. . . ."

"It's true, all right; you and I both know it. You think I don't hear what they say about me behind my back?" Val lowered her voice to a masculine pitch. "'Hey, man, how far'd you get with Val last night? Hey, have her take you to the Ritz, man, her daddy'll pay for it.'"

Emma said nothing. She watched as Val grimaced and took a deep breath.

"It's okay, though." Smiling blandly, Val went on. "I mean, I know about it, I deal with it. So I really do understand about Daniel, why you didn't want to share him. It would feel *so* nice to be special to somebody that way."

"But you are special to somebody," Emma said.

Val gave her a look, then laughed. "I meant somebody besides you."

"I'm not talking about me. I'm talking about Charlie."

Val's eyes widened. She let go of Emma's shoulders and laughed louder. "Oh, Em, this time I think Charlie's right about you—you *are* out of your mind—"

"No, I mean it. The other day I was going through his desk, and he had this picture of you when we were at the beach last summer. And when I found it, he looked really embarrassed and tried to pretend *I'd* hidden it there." Emma thought a moment, then added, "I think Charlie's been interested in you for a long time. He just didn't want anyone to know."

Val's smile was fading now. Her expression seemed almost wistful.

"You're really serious?" Val asked her.

"And I know you've been interested in him," Emma added matter-of-factly.

"No, that's not—"

"True. Yes, it is." Emma gave a firm nod. "I've always known, and it's okay. I know you didn't want me to think you were friends with me just 'cause of Charlie." Reaching for Val, Emma drew her close in another hug. "And I don't, Val. I never thought that, and I don't think that now."

For a moment the girls clung to each other. It was Val who finally pulled away again, brushing tears from her own cheek and then from Emma's.

"But . . . but this Daniel guy," Val reminded her gently. "I mean—and trust me, I can't even believe I'm sitting here saying this—but he's a *ghost*, Em. And he sure doesn't seem all that safe to be around. If what the Miss Lobergs say is true—"

"You've got to promise you won't tell Charlie about that part," Emma insisted, suppressing a shudder. Even thinking about it now chilled her all the way through. "Not the part about me having to die."

"But—"

"You can tell him I went to see the Loberg sisters, and about their connection with Betsey, and how they don't think Emma really died in the fire, if you want. But not about the box and the note." She frowned and chewed thoughtfully on her bottom lip. "If Charlie knew, he'd freak out. He might even tell Mom, and they'll—oh, who knows what they might do? The point is, if they get involved I won't be able to help Daniel, and I've *got* to help him, Val. No matter how crazy and unreal this all seems, I've *got* to find out why he's here."

Val conceded with a halfhearted nod. She wrapped her arms about herself and began to rock slowly, her brow creased in thought.

"Maybe there's another way," she said at last. "Another way we can solve this thing."

Emma looked hopeful. "What're you thinking?"

"We could hold a séance."

24

∽◌◌◌∾

"So *what* are you trying to get me to do?" Charlie stopped in his tracks, his arms full of firewood, and stared up at both girls standing on the porch.

"A séance," Val said for the third time. "Is something wrong with your hearing?"

"My hearing's fine. *I'm* fine. You, on the other hand, are completely and totally insane. In fact, I think you're as bad as *she* is."

Charlie tossed a scowl in Emma's direction while Val gazed at him calmly.

"And I think if you want this thing solved in a positive, constructive, nonviolent manner," she informed him, "then you'd better shut up and help us out."

Charlie opened his mouth and closed it again. Swearing deeply under his breath, he tossed the logs up onto the porch, then turned to face his sister.

"And you're telling me you went to the crazy old Lobergs, and they actually *knew* about all of this?"

"Yes," Emma answered. "And you were right about Emma getting out of the fire that night—or at least that's what the sisters believe. That's why Daniel's come back—he's so miserable living without her."

"Oh, I'm sorry," Charlie quipped. "I didn't think he was *living* at all."

"He just loves her so much!" Val felt Emma's elbow in her side and added quickly, "I mean—*loved* her so much!"

"Hmmm." Charlie regarded the two of them with narrowed eyes. "And the Miss Lobergs told you if you contacted Daniel, he'd go away and leave you alone?"

The girls exchanged secret glances. Both of them nodded.

"Well, it's worth a try, isn't it?" Val insisted, while Emma moved down the steps and planted herself squarely in Charlie's path.

"See, Charlie, this proves I'm not crazy. The sisters knew all about Daniel and Emma and what happened to them—they'd heard it all from Betsey."

Charlie looked blank. "Who's Betsey?"

"The housekeeper, don't you remember? In the picture? The one with the apron? Betsey helped Daniel and Emma arrange secret meetings, and she knew everything. She's related to the Miss Lobergs, some cousin or something. So what's happening *is* real. They said so."

"Oh, well!" Charlie rolled his eyes and flung his arms wide. "Well, then of *course* if the Miss Lobergs said so—"

"And besides that, they think you're quite the stud."

Charlie broke off midsentence, his mouth still open.

"Better be careful, Charlie," Val teased. "No more undressing in front of your bedroom window. You never know how many little old ladies are out there waiting for the show." She paused, then added innocently, "Come to think of it, you'd better be more careful about taking showers, too."

Charlie's cheeks flushed. "You two're sick," he muttered.

Ignoring their banter, Emma grabbed his sleeve. "So when's the séance?"

"If the anniversary of the fire is tomorrow, I say we better do it quick," Val spoke up. "The quicker the better. In fact, I say we do it tonight."

Charlie shook his head and tried to pry Emma from his jacket. "Look, how do we know it's even gonna work?"

"It'll work." Emma traded another quick glance with Val. "It *has* to work." *My whole life might depend on it.* For the hundredth time she told herself she didn't really believe it. For the hundredth time she felt terrified that it actually could be true.

"But what if it doesn't?" Charlie persisted stubbornly. "I think we're in way over our heads here, and we all know it—"

"It's decided, then," Val interrupted. "We do it tonight. Darkness is more conducive to the spirit world."

Charlie threw her a wry glance. "And who made you the expert?"

"I happen to know a lot about séances," Val defended herself. "Remember when I interviewed that medium for the school paper?"

"Who turned out to be a big fake?"

Val made a face at him. Even Emma had to smile.

"Darkness is better," Val repeated. "And three is a nice magical number."

"Well, why don't we just invite the Lobergs then, while we're at it?" Irritated, Charlie grabbed Emma's wrist and wrenched it from his jacket. "That'd make it a nice *crazy* number."

Val paused a moment, one eyebrow raised. Then very deliberately she put her hands on her hips and frowned. "Charlie, are you going to cooperate or not? We *have* to do this. We have to do this for Emma—"

"Don't you think I know that!" Charlie's outburst was so sudden that both girls jumped back. "And what if something goes wrong? Has either one of you even *considered* the possibility that something worse could happen? I mean, this spirit stuff is nothing to fool around with. What if something goes wrong and Emma gets hurt?"

The two girls stared at him. Emma felt a cold chill tighten around her heart, and she slipped her arm through Val's. Charlie's face was a taut mixture of anger and concern, and she could see a muscle working fiercely in his jaw.

"I'm just saying . . ." Charlie drew a deep, slow breath and let it out again. "I just don't want anything bad to happen. That's all."

Without even thinking, Emma reached out again for his arm. Charlie pulled away.

"Maybe Daniel's just sort of trapped," Val said softly. "You know . . . between this world and the next. Maybe he's still too connected to the people and places he loved when he was here."

Charlie shrugged his shoulders. He gave his sister a sidelong glance. "Which means . . . Emma."

"Exactly. Which means Emma. So the way I see it, all we have to do is convince Daniel he's dead."

"And how do you plan to do that?" Charlie's tone was mocking. "Hey, Dan, you need to get on with your life, buddy! Oh—sorry—I mean, your *afterlife*!"

Val wasn't amused. "We'll just tell him, okay? God, Charlie, do you think you could be any more of a pain—"

"*I* should tell him," Emma broke in. "I seem to be the one Daniel's connected to, so I should be the one to tell him."

"I don't like it," Charlie muttered. "I don't like it at all."

Val's patience had reached its end. Releasing Emma's arm, she marched determinedly down the porch steps. She stopped eye-level with Charlie and glared at him. "You have a better suggestion?"

"Well, what if we're just adding fuel to the fire?" Charlie shot back. "I mean, what if the more we *humor* this whatever-he-is, the more demanding he gets? Maybe if we just ignore him—"

Emma was incredulous. "You think he'll just go away? Oh, that's great, Charlie—that is such classic guy-logic!"

"And you still don't know what you're dealing with! You and Emma act like this is just some stupid romance novel where everyone's gonna live happily ever after! I'm telling you there's something *wrong* here—something *bad*—I can *feel* it! From everything I've heard about that day, Daniel promised Emma he'd save her. Well, he *did* save her; he *kept* his promise. Emma managed to get out, and *he* died, so why's he still hanging around?"

"Charlie, you don't know anything about love!" Val snapped at him. "You don't have the slightest clue what the power of love can do!" Her eyes were blazing, and as Charlie leaned in closer to her face, she leaned in even closer to his. "Daniel's still here because he and Emma got *separated*. They always planned to be together, in life *and* in death! So if Emma tells him to go away, then maybe he'll go."

"You think he'll go, Val? Well, think about this! What if he *does* go, but he just decides to take *this* Emma with him—"

"Oh, for God's sake—stop it!" Emma shouted. *You know, don't you, Charlie? You know what could happen, even though I didn't tell you, you already know.* Working her way in between them, she shoved Val and Charlie apart. "Stop arguing and let's just do it, okay? This isn't solving anything!"

The other two regarded her sheepishly. Without another word, Val resumed her lofty position on the porch, and Charlie backed off, thrusting his hands deep into the pockets of his jeans. Emma stared down at the ground, willing her emotions into some semblance of order, trying to slow the pounding in her brain.

Hold on, Em, get a grip—nothing's gonna happen, the Miss Lobergs are crazy, you're not in any danger, you're not gonna die, don't even think about dying. . . .

"So where should we hold the séance?" She spoke again, more calmly this time, and she could see Charlie watching her, studying her, even though she tried to clear all the turmoil from her mind. "The Miss Lobergs might see us if we try and use their garden."

Charlie seemed resigned, even though his gaze remained firmly on her. "Why can't we just have it in our own living room?"

"Don't be ridiculous," Val chided. "We have to do it where everything started, where the emotions are still really strong."

"Oh, come on, you can't be serious about going back to that house—"

"Well, of course the house!" Val's smile bordered on smugness. "The house is perfect. Emma's seen Daniel in the house, and that's where a lot of their best memories are."

"No way. There is *no way* I'm gonna let Emma go back inside that house—"

"We have to, Charlie," Emma said quickly. "Val's right—I think that's our best chance of contacting him."

"But—"

"If I don't go to Daniel, he might come looking for *me*. Is that what you want?"

Once more Charlie's jaw tightened. Emma could see the outline of his hands curling slowly into fists.

"This is crazy," he grumbled. "This is insane. God, I can't believe we're standing here talking about this like it's—it's—"

"Normal? No, Charlie, it's not normal—but it is *real*. It *is* happening. And we're the only ones who can stop it."

Charlie stared at her. She could see the worry in his

eyes; she could hear his sigh as he ran one hand back through his hair.

"So we call him up." Charlie nodded grudgingly. "And then what happens?"

Val sounded proud of herself. "We've got it all planned. Emma tells him she loves him. She gives him back the ring. And then he goes away."

"But she's not really his Emma," Charlie argued.

"But she was then." Val was growing impatient again. "And Daniel thinks she is now, so that's all that matters. Problem solved."

"Just like that."

"Yes. Just like that."

That grunt of disgust again, deep in Charlie's throat. He trudged up the steps, shouldered past Val, and opened the kitchen door. He cast a look back at them over his shoulder.

"Seven o'clock. Mom's going over to Aunt Joan's tonight, and I don't want her here asking questions."

"Seven," Val affirmed.

"And not a single word to anyone."

The girls nodded solemnly.

Slipping one arm around Emma, Val tried her best to sound confident. "Don't worry, Charlie. We're doing the right thing."

"You think so?" Charlie's troubled blue eyes looked deep into hers. "Then how come it feels so wrong?"

25

∽✺∾

"I guess we're ready," Emma said, rummaging through her backpack. "I think I've got everything we need."

"What about a dustpan?" Charlie asked blandly. "You know, so we'll have something to put him in when he turns to ashes?"

"He's not a vampire," Emma grumbled. "And don't you dare ruin this, Charlie."

"Hey, don't lecture me—I'm not gonna ruin anything." Charlie pulled a flashlight from the kitchen drawer and flicked it on, shining it full on Emma's face. As she put up a hand to shield her eyes, Charlie turned the beam off, then on again, then off. Scowling, Emma grabbed for it, but Charlie whisked it out of her reach.

"Charlie, I mean it! This is serious!"

"I know this is serious, Em, and I'm being a good sport about it." Charlie feigned innocence. "You and

Val obviously know what you're doing. You'll get no problems from me."

Once more he aimed the flashlight into her face; once more Emma made a grab for it. She was still in the process of wrestling it away from him when the back door opened, letting Val in on an icy blast of wind.

"It's starting to snow." Val shivered. She'd brought a flashlight of her own, clutched in one mittened hand, and her cheeks were bright with cold. Her hair had worked free from the edges of her wool cap, ringing her face with dark curls.

Emma felt Charlie's grip loosen. She pulled away from him just in time to catch the expression on his face as he stared at Val. *Oh, my God, Charlie, you are so hopelessly in love.* He glanced at her, startled, then hurriedly busied himself at the kitchen sink.

Val was staring, too, Emma noted. Taking in the full length of Charlie's backside, from his shaggy hair, to his baggy blue sweater, to his faded jeans, to his muddy hiking boots. As Charlie turned around without warning, Val cleared her throat and gestured toward the door.

"It's starting to snow," she said lamely for the second time.

"Thanks for the weather report. Twice," Charlie teased, deadpan.

Emma sighed. "Shut up, Charlie."

"You don't have to go," Val informed him primly. "I'm sure Emma and I can manage just fine without you."

Charlie's tone was all seriousness. "But I might get scared staying here all alone. I better go along so you two can protect me."

Bundled against the cold, they cut across the backyard and climbed over the fence. No one spoke as they neared the Farmington house. The beams from their flashlights shone uselessly against the smothering shadows of night, and the sky was rapidly thickening with huge soft flakes of snow. As Emma watched the old house looming ominously before them, she thought it had never looked so somber, so tragically sad.

So haunted . . .

At the front steps the three of them paused. It was Charlie who walked up onto the porch and knocked loudly on the door.

"Acme Exorcisms!" he shouted. "We're here to spirit away your spirits!"

"That's not funny!" There was a faint quiver in Val's voice, and Emma quickly squeezed her hand.

"She's right, Charlie—don't joke about it. You might make things worse."

Charlie turned to face them, his expression grave. "What? Are you saying my approach is . . . disrespectful? How insensitive of me." He thought a minute, then banged again. "Demon Exterminators! We're here to—"

"Stop it, Charlie!"

Emma glared up at her brother, then turned her attention back to Val. She could feel her friend trembling, and she gave Val's hand another quick squeeze.

"Sorry." Val looked almost embarrassed. "I've never been this close to the house before. It's a lot different seeing it from the street."

Emma was sympathetic. "I know—it's ten times creepier. And for your information," she continued stiffly, addressing Charlie, "Daniel is *not* a demon. He's gentle and protective."

"Right. Just your typical friendly, lovelorn spirit."

"He tried to save my life," Emma said angrily. "And died trying. I owe him that."

Charlie's look was incredulous. "You don't owe him anything! You don't even know the guy—you weren't there—you don't belong here—you—"

"Shh!" Val held up both hands, her voice sharp. "If you're going to make fun of this, we don't want you here, Charlie. I mean it. This is very serious."

"He knows it's serious," Emma assured her. "He always acts stupid like this when he's scared."

Before Charlie could answer, Val hurried up the steps and took hold of the door. She started to turn the knob, but he put a restraining hand on her arm.

"Wait, Val. Let me go first."

This time Val didn't argue. For a brief second their eyes locked and held before Charlie slipped inside.

Emma stared at the spot where Charlie'd been standing. Frowning slightly, she glanced back toward the lawn, then scanned the deep shadows along the porch.

"What's wrong?" Val whispered.

Emma shook her head. As her eyes focused upon the door, an icy chill began to crawl through her veins. *No, Charlie . . . no . . .*

"Don't let him go in there, Val," she said suddenly. "Make him come out."

Val looked confused. "What?"

"I don't know. . . ." Emma came slowly up the steps and reached out for her friend. "Something . . . I don't know. I've changed my mind. I don't think we should be doing this—"

"Of course we should be doing this. We've already

had this discussion! I thought we all agreed—"

"Well, I don't agree now. I want Charlie to leave. *Please*, Val, make him come out—"

"It's too late." Worriedly, Val scanned Emma's face. "You'll never get him out of there now—it's a point of honor. Come on, it'll be fine. We're doing the right—"

"No. No, we're not." As Emma's voice tightened, she clamped harder on Val's arm. "Charlie was right, Val—this doesn't feel good to me—it feels all wrong—"

"But, Em—"

"It's me Daniel's involved with! I should go in alone."

"I won't let you do that—and I *guarantee* you Charlie won't."

"Charlie," Emma insisted, still trying to make Val understand. "We've got to get him out of there, it's not safe. And you shouldn't go in, either."

"Em—"

But Emma pushed past her into the darkened hall.

"Charlie?" she called anxiously. "Charlie, where are you?"

Had he answered? The silence was so thick, so overwhelming, it felt like shadows echoing over and over through her head.

Emma walked cautiously through the foyer, playing her flashlight over the walls. Behind her she heard Val coming through the door, and somewhere in the distance she thought she heard Charlie's voice, speaking softly. The beam of Val's flashlight joined hers in a wide, slow arc, revealing the same empty corners and bare floors, the layers of cobwebs and dust. The girls looked nervously at each other, their breath hanging in the stale, frosty air. The cold was bone-chilling. As Val stumbled and caught herself, her cry echoed mockingly back at them.

"You okay?" Emma whispered.

"Yeah. Sorry."

"Stay close to me."

"Where's Charlie?"

"In here, I think."

Emma walked ahead, her attention suddenly caught by a wide open doorway to their left. Pausing on the threshold, she recognized the parlor at once—but a parlor much changed since her last unearthly visit. There were no rich furnishings, no comforting lamplight, no heavy draperies to shut in their secrets. Now there was only the fireplace, a gaping hole of crumbling brick and stone, to mark the spot where she and Daniel had loved once upon a time. Charlie was leaning in front of that fireplace, both arms propped on the mantel, and his face was pensive as he watched them come in.

"I want you both to go," Emma ordered them. "I want to contact Daniel by myself."

Val turned on her instantly. "Don't even think about it! We're not going to leave you here!" Then, as Charlie remained silent, "*Are* we, Charlie?"

Charlie seemed to rouse himself with an effort. In the dim glow of their flashlights, his skin shone unnaturally pale.

"Tell her, Charlie!" Val was adamant. "Tell her she's not staying here by herself!"

"This place is so strong," Charlie murmured.

Startled, Emma took a step toward him. His face was expressionless, yet she could feel his fear and dismay, she could feel his stunned realization of what was happening.

"Please go, Charlie," she whispered.

But he only continued to watch her. He watched as she pleaded at him with her eyes and with her thoughts. He watched as Val pressed close against her side.

"What is it?" Val demanded. "What do you mean? Come on, guys—stop it. You're being too weird."

Slowly Charlie shook his head. His lips tightened in a grim smile.

"I'm not leaving you, Em," he said quietly.

For a long moment Emma looked back at him. Despite his growing fear, the surge of Charlie's protectiveness nearly overwhelmed her; his resolve was like stone. She could tell he understood the enormity of the danger now, and she opened herself to his strength.

At last she nodded.

"This is it, then," she announced. "This is where we have the séance." As she dropped her pack onto the floor, Val moved back and gave her a wary look.

"Are you sure?"

"Of course I'm sure."

"Something happened just now, didn't it?" Val sounded almost eager, glancing back and forth between the twins. "I saw it—something psychic with you and Charlie—"

"You can interview us about it later, Val—we have more important things to worry about."

Together they emptied the contents of the bag. While Emma spread out a blanket on the floor, Val began lighting candles and placing them around the room. Charlie stood silently, hands thrust deep in his pockets, looking as if he wanted to be anywhere else in the world but where he was.

"Okay." Val gave the parlor one last inspection and added, "I think that's it. Everyone sit down."

Before anyone could move, a blast of snow shook the house, rattling the windowpanes and sending a mournful howl through the eaves. The candles guttered wildly. As the flames struggled to revive, the girls positioned themselves on the floor, while Charlie took his own place between them. The three sat without speaking. Val put a candle in the center of their little circle, and uneasily they all joined hands.

Charlie's palms were sweating. His eyes were fixed on Emma, his hands clasped securely with hers on his left, with Val's on his right. Candle glow flickered eerily across their faces, sending ribbons of jaundiced light into every corner of the floor and ceiling. The temperature seemed to drop another ten degrees.

Shivering violently, Val huddled into her coat. "Okay," she whispered at last. "Go ahead."

Emma looked uncertain. "What should I say?"

"Call him. Tell him . . . you know . . . that he's dead." Val thought a moment, then added, "And even though they didn't die together in the barn that night, the *real* Emma's dead now anyway, so he can just go back . . . home and find her there. Wherever that is."

Emma nodded. She squeezed Val's fingers, took a deep breath, then slowly let it out.

"Daniel," she began, her voice low. "Daniel Frye . . . are you here?"

Silence. An ominous silence, even deeper than before. A silence so malevolent that Emma suddenly gasped and began talking faster.

"Daniel, please answer me. It's Emma."

We shouldn't have come. . . . I should have known better. . . . I never should have brought them here. . . . Her thoughts were racing; she was having trouble keeping them under control. Her throat was dry as sandpaper. She ran her tongue nervously over her lips and tried even harder to concentrate.

"Daniel. Daniel, it's Emma. Can you hear me?"

But still only the silence. Emma felt the fine hairs prickling at the back of her neck; her mind swirled with shadows.

"Daniel. Please. I need to talk to you." Helplessly she glanced at Val and saw her friend nod.

"Don't give up," Val encouraged. "Just keep saying his name."

"Or better yet, let's end this thing and go home." Charlie tried to stand, but Val tightened her hold on him, forcing him back down. "Look, this isn't getting us anywhere!" he tried to reason with her. "This is stupid! Even if he *does* recognize Emma's voice, he's not gonna appear in front of a crowd! And I'm not leaving Emma here by herself. So let's just go!"

"Well, he's *sure* not going to show himself if you keep carrying on!" Val scolded. "You're ruining the mood, Charlie—just settle down and keep quiet!"

But Emma scarcely heard them now. She squeezed her eyes shut and forced her mind into sharper focus—*Daniel's face . . . his voice . . . his hands on my skin . . . the passion of his kiss . . .*

"I know you've been trying to reach me," she murmured, and her voice was so soft now, almost as if she weren't really speaking at all, only saying the words somewhere deep, deep within herself. . . . "I just want you to know I miss you. . . . I just want you to know I love you. . . . I'm here for you. . . . Please come to me. . . ."

Opening her eyes, she stared into the large flame of the center candle. She could see the piercing brightness of its light, calming her, hypnotizing her; she could feel that brightness suddenly warming her, seeping into her soul, filling her with fire and shining power.

And she heard him then. The sound of his voice so clear, so unmistakable, that it resounded through her entire being.

"Nothing will happen to me, as long as I have you. . . ."

"You still have me, Daniel," she whispered.

From some remote part of herself she could see Val looking at her so strangely, she could see Charlie's mouth opening in a soundless cry. She frowned and stared back at them, their figures so close yet so distant. *Who are these people? Who are these strangers sitting here on the floor of my parlor . . . ?*

"You still have me, Daniel," she said again, and the blond young man she didn't recognize was shouting at her now, frantic words she couldn't hear; and the young woman with the dark hair looked so frightened, so terrified. . . .

"You'll always have me!" Emma swore.

A freezing gust of air swept the room. From nowhere and everywhere at once came a low moan, a sound of such anguish and despair that Emma's heart felt torn from her breast. She held out her arms as if she could gather all the pain into herself, and tears streamed down her cheeks.

"I love you!" she gasped. "They can't separate us—they *mustn't* separate us—"

Her words were lost as lips pressed upon hers, a kiss both fierce and desperate. Through a hazy fog she could see the two unfamiliar people on either side of her, but they were beginning to fade now, their pale, frightened faces shimmering weakly in the mist.

"Who are you?" Her voice trembled with rage and she leaned forward, confronting them. "What are you doing in my house!" And yet some part of her seemed to know the true reason for their visit, some part of her sensed the imminent danger—

"My father sent you, didn't he! To keep us apart!" Emma struggled to her feet, her hands clenched in rage. "Well, it won't work—we won't be separated! Go away! We don't want you here!"

"Emma!" To her horror, the young man was shouting at her, lunging for her, trying to capture her in his arms. "*Tell* him, Emma! Tell him he has to go on without you!"

"Go away! You don't belong here! *Go away and leave us alone!*"

As Emma jerked out of reach, the young man's eyes suddenly widened and rolled back in his head. She could see his hands working frantically at his throat, his skin turning dark red, the deep marks of someone else's fingerprints forming along his windpipe. The dark-haired woman screamed as something struck violently at her shoulders and hurled her to the floor.

Emma stood by silently and watched. The young

man wasn't struggling anymore; he gave only the weakest of sighs as his knees buckled beneath him. The young woman was sobbing hysterically. As her male companion slumped forward, he spoke to her in one last whisper.

"Help me . . . Val . . . something . . . something bad . . ."

Quietly, one by one, the candles went out.

26

"Don't worry, Emma, they can't hurt us."

Daniel's voice echoed ghostly in the chilled air, in the deep pitch blackness of the room. It echoed, and then it faded, so that for a brief second Emma wondered if she was completely alone. The possibility wasn't frightening to her; rather she felt strangely comforted that the unwelcome intruders had gone. She listened, but heard no trace of them remaining. There was only the faint patter of snowflakes against the windowpanes . . . the low whine of wind around the eaves. And then, from somewhere off to her left, the slow, measured tread of footsteps.

She knew those footsteps. She'd memorized their sound, had longed to hear them every second in every day, planned every waking breath around them—measured her happiness, her salvation by their approach, measured her pain with their departure. . . .

"Emma! No!"

Without any warning, another voice cried out to her—a voice unknown and yet familiar—sending shock waves through her brain. Emma's hands flew to her temples, trying to hold the violent dizziness at bay. The voice was not outside of her, she realized, but from inside her head. Moaning softly, she squeezed her fingers tighter, and the pressure began to ease.

For just a moment the room glowed with light, before plunging once again into darkness. The footsteps halted beside her. There was a rustle of movement, and the air stirred gently upon her cheek.

"Daniel," she whispered.

And she felt him then, pressed against her, his lips whispering into her ear, his breath slow and warm down the side of her neck.

"You're mine, Emma," he murmured. "Nothing will ever take you from me again."

Emma closed her eyes. He was kissing her forehead, her nose, her cheeks, and as tears gathered beneath her eyelids, he placed his hands gently upon either side of her face.

"Look at me," he said softly. "Look here in my eyes."

Slowly Emma opened hers. In the impossible darkness of their surroundings, Daniel's eyes shone back at her, faint pinpricks at first, tiny points of strange black light, but so intense that they actually seemed to smolder as she watched. To Emma's amazement they began to grow larger, larger and blacker still, until she felt herself being pulled forcibly into their depths. She tried to blink, tried to back away, but something was happening that she couldn't stop—a subtle shifting of walls and floors, the parlor transforming around her.

"What's happening?" Emma cried. "Daniel, where are you?"

But Daniel's eyes drew back from her now, back into the silent shifting of the room. And as panic rose inside her, the light that had been Daniel's eyes now burst full around her in an explosion of flames.

"Don't let go of me, Emma! Hold tight to my hand!"

And she could see him now, in the barn, the murky outline of his face through black waves of smoke, and she could hear his voice, gasping and weak, barely audible beneath the groan and crash of collapsing timbers—

"You've got to stay conscious!" he begged her. "We're almost there!"

She realized he was dragging her, that he was crawling across the floor and pulling her with him, even as tongues of flame swept in at them from every side, licking up the walls and eating away at the overhead rafters. Blind and choking, Emma struggled to keep up, but there was so much smoke, so much blood, blood everywhere and she was soaked with it, her long skirts wet and red, Daniel's blood flowing and flowing as his grip on her began to loosen and the last of his strength drained away. . . .

"We're going to make it, Emma!" he promised. "I'm going to get you out of here!"

"I can't do it! I can't breathe—"

"Yes, you can! There's a boarded up window back here! It's big enough to crawl through, but it's high and you'll have to climb!"

"Then go! Go without me!"

"I'll boost you up! Emma, do you hear? Stay close to me! I have to knock out these boards and—"

His words were lost, drowned by a sudden roar of flames. As Emma screamed and rolled away, she felt the scorching heat, heard the deafening crash, and she saw him turn, for one brief instant she saw his eyes, the shock and the horror, the wild, infinite love as they gazed at her for the last time. And then the roof was caving in, everything collapsing around her, crushing her, burning her, burying her alive—

"*Daniel!*" she shrieked.

Terror—panic—the smell of burnt flesh—my flesh!—shrieks of agony—my pain!—and darkness descending upon her, the deep, merciful silence . . .

"I'm dead," Emma murmured. "Oh, God . . . I'm dead. . . ."

"*No!*"

From that distant, unreachable place she heard him cry for her, mourn for her, but there was no hope now . . . no hope.

"*Emmmmaaa!*"

"*Emma!*" And the voice became two voices now, two very different and distinct voices, voices speaking close by as if they knew her well.

Emma struggled to open her eyes. Without warning a glare of light burst on in her face, and she immediately began thrashing at it.

"No, Emma, no! Wake up!"

A woman's voice. A voice she recognized.

"Betsey?" she whispered. "Oh, Betsey, you're the only one I can trust—"

"Wake up, Em!" The voice sounded desperate and tearful. "Please wake up! Can you hear me?"

There was no fire. No smoke, no screams, no helpless terror.

There was only a flashlight.

And Val kneeling beside her, clutching Emma within the tight circle of her arms.

"It wasn't me," Emma mumbled, and she looked up into Val's face, her words and thoughts still rambling. "It wasn't me that night—I thought it was, but it *wasn't*, it wasn't me. . . ."

"Emma! Stop it! Stop it *now*!"

Emma's body went limp as Val shook her fiercely by the shoulders. She glanced around in confusion and said again, "It wasn't—"

"Please, Emma! You've got to listen!"

"But I'm trying to tell you—"

"And I'm trying to tell *you* that Charlie's hurt! We've got to get him out of here, and you've got to help!"

Very slowly Emma shook her head. The room came into hazy focus around her, candles still flickering, shadows still crouching along the walls. But something was different—dangerously different, she could feel it—and this time when she peered into Val's face, she saw the raw terror there.

"Where's Charlie?" she demanded. "What happened?"

"I don't know." Val's tone bordered on hysteria. "I don't know! Something bad. Something horrible!"

Emma got unsteadily to her feet. She could see Charlie now, lying on the floor just beyond reach of the light, and as she hurried over to him, Val shone the flashlight onto his face. He was deathly pale, and his cheeks and throat were covered with cuts and dark, ugly bruises.

"Oh, God." Emma dropped down beside him and put a cautious hand to his forehead. "Charlie . . ."

Her brother moaned softly. Val swallowed a frightened sob and knelt beside the twins.

"How'd this happen?" Emma murmured. "Who did this to him?" She stared at Val in dismay. She'd never seen her best friend like this before. Gasping and trembling, Val was starting to come apart right in front of her.

"I don't know, Em—oh, God, I don't—"

"You know who did it, Emma." Weakly, Charlie lifted his head. He tried to shift his weight but moaned again, louder this time. "Damn . . . I think something's broken."

"Charlie sensed it, and so did you!" Val insisted wildly. "We should never have come—I'll never forgive myself!"

Charlie grimaced in Val's direction. "I'll never forgive you, either."

"Oh, Charlie!" Val wailed, and he looked instantly contrite.

"Val. Val, I'm *kidding*."

"Don't listen to him, Val, it wasn't your fault." As Val's eyes brimmed with tears, Emma put a comforting hand on her arm. "I was the one who wanted to go through with it."

"Okay," Charlie mumbled, his old sarcasm struggling through. "Then *you're* the one I'll never forgive."

Emma ignored him. Rocking back on her heels, she ran a critical gaze around the perimeters of the room.

"But whatever was here is gone now," she said. "Can't you feel it? It's different from when we came in."

"So let's go while we still can," Charlie groaned. "I'd hate to wear out our welcome."

"I sensed something, but I just didn't think it'd be like this," Emma admitted. "I didn't think it'd be this *bad*, I didn't think I'd be gone so long."

Charlie's face blanched against a fresh wave of pain. "What do you mean?"

"I mean, I went back there. I saw what happened. I was gone a long time."

"No way. Two whole minutes, maybe. Three at the most."

"He's right, Em," Val said. She'd calmed down a little now, and her voice sounded steadier. Emma saw that Charlie had taken Val's hand. "The second Charlie hit the floor, you came out of your trance, or whatever it was."

Bewildered, Emma stared at her brother. She stared at his bruises and the streaks of dirt on his face and the smear of blood on his cheeks.

"He really hates me, your boy Daniel." Charlie's expression was grave. "He wouldn't let me through to you. It's obvious he hates *anyone* who comes between you and him. Whether it's now or a hundred years ago—"

"But it *was* a hundred years ago," Emma broke in anxiously. "That's what I'm trying to tell you. I was back there—back to that night—back to the fire."

"Well, you were somewhere," Val agreed, giving a

deep shudder. "I couldn't wake you up. It was like you couldn't hear me or see me—like you were dead."

For a long moment Emma was silent. Then very quietly she said, "I *was* dead."

She saw the stunned expression on Val's face, the shock in Charlie's eyes.

"We've been wrong about everything," she said miserably. "It wasn't Emma who escaped the fire that night. It was Daniel."

27

❧

"So now what do we do?"

As Val eased her car out of the hospital parking lot, she glanced quickly over at Emma. Emma's face was a rigid silhouette, and in the seat behind them, Charlie slumped silently against the door with his right arm in a sling.

"I don't know, Val," Emma said hollowly. "I haven't had time to think it all through."

Val squinted hard at the windshield. "Yeah, well, just be glad your mom's snowed in at your aunt's house—that's all I can say. God, this storm is terrible."

"I wish they hadn't made me call her. She's *really* gonna freak out when she sees how bad Charlie looks. A broken collarbone . . . and of all nights for *your* dad to be on duty in the emergency room—"

"Don't remind me," Val cut her off. "But at least he

got Charlie in and out without your mom having to be there. And I think he believed us about Charlie falling down the stairs. Let's hope so anyway."

"We'll just have to remember to keep all our stories straight." Emma ran a weary hand across her forehead. "Don't forget to stop at the drugstore; I need to get Charlie's pain pills."

Val's smile was humorless. "I wish we could just buy a pill to make Daniel go away."

The weather had gotten much worse since they'd left the Farmington house. Snow fell even thicker, gusting wildly along the streets on a bitter wind, only now it was mixed with ice. As Val wiped impatiently at the fogged-up glass, she caught another glimpse of Charlie in her mirror. Despite the sedative a nurse had given him at the hospital, he was obviously still in intense pain. Dark circles hollowed his eyes, and he stared out into the swirling night, looking even more depressed than he had before.

"Hey, you," she teased him. "I know the doc said no sports for a while, but look at it this way. You'll have all the girls feeling sorry for you, and wanting to help with your homework, and carry your books and stuff."

Charlie wasn't impressed. "What happened back there?" he asked flatly.

The two girls looked at each other.

"Come on, you guys." Charlie frowned. "We have to talk about it. This is bigger than anyone can handle. We have to decide what to do."

Without a word Val eased the car toward the curb in front of the drugstore. Then she shifted into park and let the motor idle while Emma turned sideways in her seat. Charlie didn't move. Val took a deep breath and went first.

"I remember the lights going out . . . and it got so cold. Just all of a sudden this freezing cold. I heard Charlie yell."

"Something attacked me." Charlie picked up the story. "It knocked me back and started twisting my arm. It had a hold of my throat, and I was trying to breathe—and the whole time I just kept bending and bending, and I knew something had to give. I heard this really loud popping sound. The pain was so bad, I think I must have blacked out for a second."

Val met his eyes in the rearview mirror, wincing at the memory. "I heard it, too. It was horrible."

"Everything went so fast. There wasn't time to even realize what was happening."

"I could hear Charlie fighting with someone. But I couldn't see who it was, and I couldn't help him. I was just . . . just so scared." Val paused and drew a deep breath. "I'm so sorry, Charlie."

"You don't have anything to be sorry about—we were all scared," Charlie admitted grudgingly. "And you couldn't have done anything, anyway. You can't fight something that's not real."

For the first time Emma spoke up. "But he *is* real. That's just the problem—he's as real as you and me. Except he exists in another dimension, and he's lost somewhere between there and here."

"We're in way over our heads," Charlie mumbled. Cautiously he shifted his weight, but the pain hit him mercilessly, making him gasp. After several seconds he added, "This isn't just some parlor game we're dealing with anymore—this is major league. And tomorrow's the anniversary of the fire. What are we gonna do?"

Val reached back and rested her hand on his good arm. "There's got to be an answer somewhere. Something we haven't thought of—"

"All we've done is think, and we're not getting anywhere! I'm tired of thinking. Will someone please go in and get my pills?"

"Don't get all worked up," Val soothed. "You'll only hurt worse."

"Thanks for the prognosis, Dr. Val," Charlie muttered, but Val turned back to Emma.

"Okay, Em, tell us again. What you saw when you were with Daniel this time."

Unhappily Emma looked down at the floor. None of them had said a word on their way to the hospital earlier; none of them had wanted to even mention tonight's horrifying events. As if they were all still dazed, still trapped in their own personal aftermaths of shock. *Charlie's right . . . we're not getting anywhere, and I can't think of anything else to try. . . .*

"Hurry up, will you?" Charlie groaned. "I need serious drugs here."

"In a minute," Val scolded him. "You can't take anything for another hour, anyway. Go on, Em."

Emma gave a reluctant nod. "It's just what I told you before. I saw what really happened that night. And it wasn't Daniel who died in the fire, like we thought—it was Emma."

"And you're *absolutely* sure?" Val prompted.

"I'm positive. When Emma thought Daniel was

dead, she wanted to die with him. I remember taking in these huge gulps of smoke, hoping I'd just pass out and not feel the fire. And I *did* lose consciousness for a minute, but–"

"Will you stop that?" Charlie burst out furiously, causing both girls to jump. "Stop saying I! It's not *you*, Emma–it wasn't *you*!–will you just stop saying that! You're making me crazy!"

"Charlie, I . . . I didn't mean to. . . ." Flustered, Emma tried to compose herself, tried once more to gather her thoughts. Val glanced worriedly toward the backseat and reached again for Charlie's arm.

"Come on, Charlie, it's okay. She *knows* she's not the other Emma–just let her tell it like she remembers."

Emma could feel Charlie seething behind her. When he didn't say anything more, she glanced at Val and cautiously went on.

"When I–I mean, Emma Farmington–came to again, Daniel was still alive, trying to save her. He remembered a boarded-up window behind some stalls, and he was dragging her to the back of the barn."

"But what about the stab wound?" Val asked. "Wasn't he dying?"

"He was still bleeding–there was blood all over Emma and all over Daniel and all over the floor. That's why he was so weak. And there wasn't any fresh air– they couldn't breathe."

Val's eyes grew sad. "So he was going to lift Emma through the opening and help her out."

"Yes, but he had to knock the boards down first. And she was so dizzy from the smoke. I remember just lying there–Emma just lying there–only I *was* Emma, I felt every single thing Emma was feeling. I'm sorry, Charlie, I can't expect you to understand when I don't even understand it myself. But I *was* there somehow—and it really *was* happening to me. I was so weak and disoriented, and Daniel told me to stay close to him. . . ."

Emma trailed off. Tears rose in her throat, and she forced them back down.

"And then the roof caved in. . . . I mean, I guess it was the roof. The hayloft, maybe. Rafters and sparks and flames just pouring down on me, like the whole sky was raining fire. And then . . . I died."

For a long moment there was silence. Finally Val whispered, "How did it feel?"

"Just . . . strange. Nothing. Peaceful, I guess. Dark."

"Were you afraid?"

"I was before; I was terrified. But after I died . . . I don't really know. I mean, that's all I remember. When I died, I was back here again. So maybe dying is like waking up from a dream. Only you wake up in a different place."

"But you didn't actually *see* Daniel get out of the barn," Charlie reminded her. "In your dream. We're still just assuming he escaped."

Emma pondered this, frowning. "I saw him looking at me right before everything started caving in. I screamed, but I never heard him answer."

"He had to have gotten out," Val insisted. "Otherwise he wouldn't be coming back now, trying to find Emma."

Charlie's expression was grim. "So the whole time Josiah had everyone out looking for Daniel, Daniel really *was* alive."

"Then where'd he go?" Emma wondered. "There were so many people out there trying to hunt him down and—"

"Don't even ask," Charlie broke in quickly. "That could end up being another whole episode."

He sounded so miserable that Val gave him a sympathetic smile. "Poor Charlie. And poor Daniel. I wonder if he had a broken shoulder like you? He must have been in terrible shape that night—he must have had to hide out somewhere till he was strong enough to get away."

"You're right, Val." Emma sat straighter, turning eagerly toward her friend. "I remember now . . . what Daniel said to Emma that night before they tried to leave. He said he knew the countryside so well, and that there were places to hide where the devil himself couldn't find them."

"Meaning not just the devil," Charlie added softly. "Meaning also Josiah Farmington."

The three of them lapsed into silence. It was Charlie who finally spoke.

"So . . . what if Josiah's suicide wasn't really a suicide at all?"

Val and Emma exchanged surprised looks. Both of them shifted around in their seats to give Charlie their full attention.

"I mean, everyone thought he was this poor grieving father," Charlie went on. "But maybe Daniel came back. Later on, when everything calmed down. Maybe Daniel came back and murdered him."

Val made a sound of disgust in her throat. "Well, I sure don't feel sorry for Josiah. I'm glad he died. In fact, I hope he suffered at the end, just like Daniel and Emma had to suffer. He deserved every bad thing he got."

"That's what I've always loved about you, Val—your sensitivity and compassion." Charlie motioned weakly toward the window. "So will somebody *please* go in now and get my—"

"It's just that I keep thinking about something else," Emma broke in. "Something else Daniel told me—I mean, told *Emma*. He said nothing would ever hurt her. He promised her nothing would ever hurt her again, and then he said, 'I swear it on my love for you.'"

"When did he say that?" Val asked.

"The same night they tried to run away. Daniel was fed up with the way Josiah treated her—it was right after he found me—*her*—in the cellar."

Val sighed. "That's so romantic."

Charlie shot her a withering glance.

"Well, it is!" Val insisted, returning the glance indignantly. "Imagine how devastated he felt when he couldn't keep his promise, and she died."

"Can we please just stick to the facts and leave out the fairy tales?" Charlie scowled, but again Emma straightened with excitement.

"Val's right, Charlie—think about it! If Daniel lived and Emma died, then he must've felt like he betrayed every single trust she ever put in him. He was supposed to be her whole life—her salvation. But when he tried to save her, it ended up being her death."

"How could you even bear that?" Val looked close to tears. "How could you even go on living after that, feeling so guilty and responsible?"

"You couldn't," Emma said softly. "At least *Daniel*

couldn't. That's why his soul can't find any peace. That's why he's come back for her!"

Val seemed lost in thought. When she finally turned to Emma, she had a strange expression on her face.

"So . . . if Emma died in the fire that night, it means she doesn't need to die again this time. Right? Which *also* means . . ."

Emma stared at her in slow realization. "The Miss Lobergs were wrong."

"What are you two talking about?" Charlie growled.

"Nothing," Emma said quickly. She pondered a moment, then gave a tense smile. "You're right, Val, there must be something else Daniel wants . . . something else that needs to happen. But *what*?"

"What about the Miss Lobergs?" Charlie persisted.

Emma shook her head impatiently. "Hush, Charlie. I'm trying to think."

Snow pattered heavily against the windows. Between the hum of the motor and the heater's soothing warmth, Emma felt the last of her strength beginning to wane. It was all making such perfect sense now—the anguish Daniel had suffered for nearly a hundred years, the unbearable burden in his heart that had kept him separated from the one he would love for eternity.

"Poor Daniel," she whispered. Her own heart felt heavy within her. Instinctively she pressed one hand against her chest, as if that simple gesture could obliterate all of Daniel's and Emma's pain. "What is it you really want from me . . . ?"

Her words trailed away. She could feel the slow, steady rhythm of her heartbeat, yet suddenly the aching began to intensify. Clutching her chest with both hands now, Emma gasped and leaned forward in surprise. She could hear her heartbeat growing louder and louder—only there were *two* heartbeats now, two perfectly matched heartbeats, pounding and echoing through her brain.

"Emma?" She saw Val's lips moving, but her friend's voice seemed miles away. "Emma, are you all right?"

Emma couldn't speak. She couldn't speak and she couldn't move, and the heartbeats went faster, faster, icy blood surging through her veins, her heart pumping out of control, ready to burst wide open. Her lips parted and she gazed helplessly at Val, and then without warning the heartbeats slowed again, slowed so rapidly, so weakly, that her whole body convulsed from the shock.

"Emma!"

She could hear Charlie's voice now, and that was Charlie's left arm around her, and Val screaming and shaking her, *shadows and whispers swirling thick through my mind, and fog rolling in, gray and endless and oh, so soft . . .*

"Emma! It's happening again, Charlie! Do something!"

Is that Val? Is that anyone I used to know?

"Help her, Charlie! Oh, God, Emma, what should I do?—oh, God—oh, God—"

"Keep talking, Val—stay with her! I'll get help!"

A door opening . . . fresh cold wind . . . wet cold snow . . . soothing . . . soothing . . .

"No," Emma murmured weakly. "No, Charlie, don't go."

Emma opened her eyes.

The car rocked gently as Charlie shut the back door again and leaned toward her between the seats. He was biting his lip, his face contorted with pain, and Val was hugging her, frantically rubbing her hands.

"This is insane, Emma!" Charlie ranted. "Insane! Do you hear me? It's got to end *now*!" He looked sick and exhausted and furiously helpless, and Val just kept rubbing Emma's hands, rubbing her hands, and whispering to her.

"What happened, Em? It was bad, wasn't it? It was really, really bad—"

"It was him," Emma said quietly, and Charlie swore and lowered his eyes from her face.

"Daniel?" Val asked.

"Yes."

"Are you sure?"

"Yes . . . yes . . ."

No one spoke. Despite the steady stream of warmth from the heater, the car was bitterly cold. Emma stared down at Val's hands and slowly pulled her own away.

"Maybe I really *don't* have a choice about any of this." She was trying to sound brave, much braver than she felt, though the quiver in her voice gave her away. "Maybe the Miss Lobergs were right, after all."

As Val's face went chalky white, Charlie's head came up again. He fixed Emma with an accusing stare.

"What are you *talking* about?" he demanded. "What aren't you telling me?"

Silently Emma gazed back at him. Val took her hands and held them once more, squeezing them gently.

"Go on, Em," Val said. "You have to tell him."

"Tell me what!" Charlie almost yelled.

"The Miss Lobergs think . . ." Emma started, then stopped. She ran her tongue over her lips and took a deep breath. "It was an oath, Charlie. A blood oath. A *deathbed* oath. Only they thought it was Emma who wrote the letter—but it was *Daniel* who wrote it."

Charlie *was* shouting now. "What are you talking about? What was the oath?"

"Betsey found Emma's treasure box in a tree. And it had a letter in it. Daniel made a vow in his own blood—that someday he'd change what he *hadn't* been able to change in his own lifetime. Don't you see?"

It was clear from Charlie's expression that he didn't see at all. Emma took another breath and went on.

"The sisters assumed from that letter that when Daniel came back this time, Emma would have to die—that was the only way she and Daniel could finally be together. Except now we know that Emma *already* died. So that leaves just one solution."

Charlie grimaced. "I know I'll seriously regret this . . . but okay. What's the solution?"

"He has to save her." It was Val who spoke up, her voice low and solemn. "That's it, isn't it? This time he has to *save* Emma. This time around it's *got* to work."

28

❦

Charlie said nothing. He ran a hand back through his hair, and his fingers trembled.

"That's crazy." When he finally spoke, he didn't even sound like himself. He closed his eyes briefly, as if gathering every ounce of strength, but his face had gone two shades paler.

"It's not crazy." Emma tried to reason with him. "It's what Daniel wants . . . what he *needs* before he can let me go."

"Do you think for one second I'd ever let you get into some situation like that?" Charlie argued. "Where you'd have to be saved? *Now?* After everything that's happened?"

Emma's look was pleading. "But didn't you see what happened just now? He had my *heart,* Charlie, he had my *life* in his total control! And you couldn't do anything about it. Just like you couldn't help me at the house tonight. He's trying to break our connection, don't you see? He's that strong!"

She thought his eyes might have gleamed with quick tears. "No," he said gruffly. "Nobody can—"

"Charlie." Emma was gentle but firm. "You *know* I'm right."

But he'd composed himself now, anger and impatience overriding the fear and pain. "Oh, come on, Em! You're just tired and upset about all this!"

"It's beyond tired and upset," Emma insisted, while Val helpfully tried to intercede.

"You're not listening to her, Charlie," Val began, but he shot her a murderous glance.

"Shut up, Val."

"Charlie, stop it," Emma scolded. "And just hear what I'm saying. Daniel's spirit and my spirit are so connected now, it's like he can reach in and take over every single part of me whenever he wants to."

She wanted to say even more, but the expression on Charlie's face stopped her. She watched as he eased himself back against the seat and stared at her as if he hated her. She knew that look—Charlie's last noble defense when he knew she was right, when he knew she'd won and he couldn't argue, when he knew she was speaking the absolute truth.

Emma stared back at him sorrowfully. "It's not my fault," she whispered.

"Of course it's not," Val soothed her, shooting an equally lethal glance back at Charlie. "Give her a break, why don't you? Hasn't she been through enough?"

"It's not my fault," Emma said again. Suddenly she wanted to cry, to jump straight out of the car and run till she couldn't run anymore. Her whole world was collapsing, yet all she could do was gaze at Charlie through tear-filled eyes and whisper, "Stop looking at me like that. I'm sorry . . . I'm sorry . . . It's not my fault. . . ."

She felt his own guilt then, overwhelming both of them, exposing itself in every line of his face. She felt his anger at himself and his thoughts spilling out at her, ashamed and remorseful. . . . *Of course it's not your fault—I'm the one who made the stupid bet with you, I'm the one who made you go to the Farmington house and spend the night. . . .*

"I'm sorry," Emma apologized yet again. She saw him lean forward; she felt his hand clumsily touch her shoulder.

"Don't be. No. It's not . . . not your fault. Just stop saying that, okay? Just . . . just . . ." He squirmed miserably, his voice getting louder. "Will someone just please go in and get my medicine before these drugs wear off?"

Val gave an exasperated sigh. "Oh, for heaven's sake, quit being such a baby. I thought you wanted us to explain about Betsey finding the box in the tree and the message written in blood and—"

"Does it even matter?" Charlie shot back. "Do I even care about this now?"

"Well, I still think I should tell you," Val insisted, "if you'll stop being a jerk for one whole minute." And she proceeded to give Charlie the remaining details of Emma's visit to the Loberg sisters. "Daniel must have had a horrible life after Emma died," she finished up. "Just a sad, empty, horrible life."

"But at least he got his revenge," Emma said softly.

Charlie scowled down at his sling. "Yeah, on me."

"You shouldn't take it personally," Val said.

"It's *my* shoulder. I consider that pretty personal."

"Maybe if you just tried talking to him again, Em." Val tried to be helpful. "You know, convince him that he really needs to let go and get on with his afterlife."

Charlie gave a snort. "Hey, call me crazy, but somehow I don't think having a heart to heart with him is the answer. I mean, we already tried that, and he didn't come off as the type you could actually *reason* with."

"But Emma was right," Val insisted. "You and I shouldn't have been there when she tried to contact him. He obviously felt threatened by us. Maybe if he and Emma were alone this time, he'd be more willing to listen."

"Absolutely, Val. He's been so *very* cooperative through all of this—"

"Well, he's a *ghost,* Charlie! He's *confused*!"

Groaning, Emma snatched the prescription from Charlie's hand. "Look, this isn't getting us anywhere. I'll just go in and get your stupid drugs, okay?"

"Now see what you did?" Charlie accused Val. "Nice work."

"What do you mean, nice work?" Val retorted. "You're the one who keeps not believing her."

Without another word Emma got out of the car and went into the drugstore, leaving Val and Charlie to stare at each other in annoyance. No one spoke when Emma came back, and they drove home in silence. After helping Charlie from the car, the girls followed him upstairs. Emma could tell his pain was getting much worse, and while Val got a glass of water from the bathroom, she quickly read the dosage on the medicine bottle and counted out two pills into Charlie's hand.

"These are potent," she warned him. "You can't take more than two at a time, remember? The doctor said they'll knock you out for about five hours."

Charlie regarded her with dull, glazed eyes. "Good. I'm looking forward to it."

He paused beside his bed and eased his arm carefully from his sling. Emma saw his sharp intake of breath, the instant drain of color from his face, and as he took hold of his T-shirt, he suddenly stared down at it in total bewilderment. Emma hid a smile, but Val's approach was much more sympathetic.

"Can't you get undressed? Do you need help?"

"Don't even think about it," Charlie shot back.

Val raised an eyebrow. "Don't flatter yourself. I'd help any poor pathetic creature with broken bones."

Before Charlie could answer, she went over to him and began working his shirt slowly up his body, carefully disentangling his left arm from his sleeve.

"Uhhh . . . I'm going downstairs," Emma said quickly, backing out of the room. Her brother's cheeks were flushed, but he didn't seem to be putting up much of a fight. "I'll be in the kitchen," Emma added. "Just in case anybody cares."

Apparently no one did. After a split-second decision not to close the door, Emma left them alone and went to put on a strong pot of coffee.

She was too restless to sit down. She felt lonely and unhappy. Everything that had happened tonight clouded her thoughts like stale smoke, hazy and clingy and disorienting. She wandered through the house, then finally stepped out onto the front porch. The snow was so thick she couldn't even see the other side of their street. Val would probably have to spend the night; already her car looked like a big white lump in the driveway.

Emma crossed her arms over her chest and huddled against the wall. What was she going to do? What *could* she do? Everything they'd managed to figure out so far was only speculative at best. The theories they'd come up with seemed reasonable, but how could they be sure? How could any of them possibly know what Daniel really wanted, what plan he had in mind for his and Emma's reunion?

"This time he has to save her."

Val's statement burned deep into Emma's brain. She saw the searing flames again. . . . She heard the desperate cries for help. . . .

Save her—but how?

Her blood ran cold at the very thought. She didn't want to be put into some fatal situation to be saved. She—Emma Donovan—wanted to wake up and find that the Farmington house had never even existed next door, that Daniel had only been a dream.

But the best dream of my life . . . a dream just for me and no one else. . . .

A stab of pain went through her. A stab of longing and sorrow and deep desire. She thought about what had happened back there in the car—the way Daniel's heartbeat had taken over her own. It had frightened her—*terrified* her—yet what horrified her now even more was that a part of her yearned for it again. Daniel's desperate need to be with her, to feel complete in her, even if it meant possessing her totally in the only way he knew how. She knew it didn't make any sense, that it could only end as it had begun—in the worst sort of tragedy. Yet it was there all the same, strong and certain in her heart.

Tears stung her eyes, and she choked them back down, because the truth was . . .

"I love you, Daniel."

She spoke the words aloud. She spoke them with passion and conviction—she couldn't help it, couldn't explain it, would never be able to understand it—she only knew with every ounce of her being that she was part of him, that her life would never be the same because of him, and no matter how hard she tried to deny it, *she* was the one he had chosen to love.

"I'll do whatever I have to," Emma promised. "Whatever it takes to—"

She jumped as the front door swung open and Val's head popped out.

"There you are! You scared me to death! I couldn't find you anywhere!"

Emma pushed past her into the warmth of the living room. "I'm surprised you even noticed."

She hated the words before they were even out of her mouth. She looked sheepishly at Val, who was watching her closely.

"Of course I noticed," Val said quietly. "We weren't up there ravaging each other, you know."

Emma gazed back at her friend. "I know," she admitted. "I don't know why I said that."

"Gosh, me neither. Does the word *stress* ring a bell?" Val slung one arm around Emma's shoulder. "But you don't have to worry, because Charlie and I have everything figured out."

"Oh. You do?"

"Yes. And actually, it's brilliant in its simplicity."

"I'm all ears."

"Well, we figure if anything's going to happen tomorrow, it will happen after dark, the way it did a hundred years ago. So you probably don't have to worry too much about staying out of buildings during the day."

"Buildings? You mean, like my *house*? *The school*?"

Val ignored her sarcasm. "Well, any place that might catch fire."

"I am *not* gonna spend tomorrow just waiting for something to happen. And I don't think the time will have anything to do with it. Whatever's supposed to happen will happen when Daniel and I are alone, and in the right place. He won't involve anyone else in this. This is between me and him."

"Exactly." Val plunged on, caught up in the excitement of their plans. "If Charlie and I are both with you, that changes the whole original scenario. It *won't* be just you and Daniel like it was that night of the fire."

"And your point is?"

"Think of it like a play. It can't have the same ending it had before if there are extra characters in it this time. Doesn't that make sense? So we'll come home with you from school. And then we'll stay with you every single minute. We won't let you out of our sight and—"

"And what? You two will protect me?" Emma's tone bordered on mockery. "You were right beside me in the car, Val, you saw what happened. Daniel can get to me anywhere if he really wants to. And I'm sure he can get rid of you and Charlie with no problem at all."

The whole plan was laughable and naive, and suddenly Emma felt more alone than ever. She shrugged Val off and turned away.

"But . . . it's worth a try, isn't it?" Val persisted, stopping her. "We only have to stick together till midnight. At midnight tomorrow the date of the fire will pass . . . the anniversary of Emma's death will be over. Daniel won't have any choice but to go back to . . . to . . . you know, his wherever . . . and then he won't come back again for another hundred years!"

She held Emma at arm's length, smiling hopefully.

"And by then you'll be dead!" she finished. "Well . . . in a non-supernatural way, I mean."

"Thanks. I feel *so* much better now. Especially with my clueless friend and my drugged, one-armed brother to protect me."

She hadn't meant to sound so harsh. She saw the wounded flicker in Val's eyes and was instantly sorry.

"It'll be fine," Val said confidently, as if Emma's remark hadn't bothered her. "I promise, Em, it *will* be. We love you. We won't let anything happen to you."

I wish I believed you, Emma thought. *You're trying so hard and I want to believe, but you don't know Daniel, you don't know him and you're no match for him. Nobody can stop him but me.*

"Okay?" Val gave her a little shake, jolting Emma from her thoughts. "So do you think the pizza place is still delivering? You'll feel a whole lot better if you eat something."

The girls went into the kitchen. Val picked up the phone and immediately frowned.

"It's dead. The storm must have knocked out the lines."

"I'm not hungry anyway. I just want some coffee."

"You sure?" Picking up the coffeepot, Val poured a cup for each of them, then promptly rattled on with her plan of action. "Maybe we shouldn't give Charlie any medicine tomorrow—so he'll be good and alert. But right now he's pretty much dead to the world."

Dead to the world . . .

Emma gave a wry smile and sat down at the table. Val leaned back against the counter and grinned.

"We got his T-shirt off, but that's as much as he'd let me help. He was actually kind of shy about it. Like I've never seen him before without his shirt?"

Emma was scarcely listening. "What?"

"Charlie. Being so modest."

"Oh. That. It's probably some male ego thing with broken bones—he gets all strange when he feels helpless. You should feel honored he even let you get that far."

"Well . . ." Val suddenly looked flustered as she walked over to the table. Sitting down, she leaned in close to Emma. "I have to tell you something, Em. We sort of got a little farther than that."

The two girls stared at each other. Val's eyes were shining and her cheeks were flushed, yet her expression bordered on guilt. Emma knew immediately what was coming.

"He kissed me," Val said. "That's all, just one kiss. I mean, not to minimize it or anything. But . . . what I mean is . . . God, can he *kiss*!"

A thousand emotions rushed through Emma, all of them painful. *I'm alone.* They hit her full force, relentlessly, like a series of physical blows. *I'm alone and I always have been, and now I'm in love with Daniel, and I'm more alone than ever. . . .*

Her heart ached within her, yet she forced a tight smile in Val's direction. "Great. I'm so glad to know Charlie has a talent for something."

Her friend hesitated, watching Emma closely. "I . . . I just wanted to tell you. I wanted you to know."

"You didn't have to. It's none of my business."

"But I wanted to."

Abruptly Emma rose from her chair. She felt depressed and confused, and the guilty look on Val's face was rapidly changing to hurt.

"I wanted to," Val said again, more cautiously this time. "That's what best friends do."

"Okay."

Emma dumped her coffee into the sink. She poured another cup.

"Okay?" Val stood up, her expression bewildered. "That's it—just okay?"

"Well, your love life's not the most important thing on my mind right now. What do you want me to say?"

Spinning around, Emma slammed her mug onto the counter. Her hands tightened into fists at her side.

"Congratulations?" she threw out. "I hope you'll be very happy? With your real live boyfriend? Who's taking you to the winter dance instead of some nightmare?

I wish I'd never made that stupid bet—you end up with Charlie, and I end up with a dead guy!"

Val looked stunned. "What are you talking about? What bet?"

"I mean . . ." Emma froze, horrified. She hadn't intended to say that, had never *wanted* to say that. But now her best friend in the whole wide world was standing there staring at her, and her mind went totally blank.

"You mean what?" Val demanded. "I don't understand."

Emma's mind was racing. Quickly she shook her head. "I don't know. I'm upset—I don't know what I'm saying."

"Yes, you do," Val accused her. "What bet? What does it have to do with me and Charlie getting together?"

"It doesn't matter. You would've ended up with him anyway—he's always been in love with you."

Val's eyes slowly filled with tears. "You did something, didn't you? Something you're not telling me. What did you do, Em?"

Miserably Emma gazed back at her. Then she lowered her head in shame.

"I didn't mean to hurt you," she mumbled. "I just wanted Charlie to ask you to the dance. And he said he would if I spent the night at the Farmington house. And that's how this all got started." She raised her eyes to Val's stricken face. "But I *swear* to you, it wouldn't have mattered—he'd have asked you anyway!"

"No!" Val snapped back at her. "He did it because he felt obligated! He did it because he lost the bet!"

"That's not true! Believe me, if Charlie hadn't wanted to ask you, *nothing* could have made him do it—not me, and especially not a stupid bet!"

"Oh, Emma, how could you do this to me? I'll *never* be able to forgive you for this! Never!"

The words sliced like knives through Emma's heart. She could see their friendship crumbling right in front of her, all the special trust they'd shared. She watched a tear slide down Val's cheek, and she reached out for her, but Val jerked away.

"Look, I know it was wrong of me," Emma begged, "but I really did mean well! I really wanted the two of you to get together! And Charlie didn't kiss you tonight because of any bet or obligation! You believe that, don't you? You *have* to believe that!"

Val's mouth opened, then closed again. Without a word she gathered her coat and purse from the chair and started for the door.

"Val, please! I'm sorry!"

Val let herself outside, then slammed the door behind her. Wrenching it open, Emma shouted after her, but Val was already getting into her car.

"What are you doing?!" Emma cried desperately. "You can't go home in this storm! Val! *Wait!* You can't even see out the windshield!"

The engine roared. As Emma ran toward the car, it skidded from the driveway and shot off down the street.

"Oh, no," Emma whispered. "Oh, Val . . . what have I done?"

29

Emma stood there for a long time.

She stood there alone on the curb, hoping Val's car would turn around, but the taillights grew fainter and fainter and finally disappeared into the snow.

Emma felt sick. Sick to her stomach and sick at heart. She couldn't believe what she'd said back there in the kitchen. She wished she could take it all back, every word of it; she wished this night had never happened. What if Val had a wreck on the way home? Following her was out of the question—Charlie's old car would never make it through this storm—and now she couldn't even use the phone to call for help. If something happened to Val, she'd never forgive herself.

It's all my fault.

She was wet and freezing. She'd run out here without a jacket, and her clothes and hair were soaked through.

Emma began to cry.

As tears raced down her cheeks, she began thinking how responsible she was for every other wrong thing that had happened. *She* was the one who'd dragged Val and Charlie into this mess. If it hadn't been for her, Charlie wouldn't be lying upstairs, all bruised and battered, and Val wouldn't be out driving recklessly on the icy roads.

All my fault.

Dejectedly Emma went inside. She was shivering violently, and her whole body ached. She curled up on the couch, pulled an afghan around her, and turned on the television. Storm updates took precedence on nearly every station. Schools were going to be closed the next day. Travel advisories were in effect. Power outages were being reported all over the city.

The clock on the bookshelf began to chime, and Emma was shocked to realize it was after midnight.

Yesterday had become today.

Our day . . . Daniel's and mine.

Only this time she wasn't going to wait for fate's intervention into her life. She was tired of being afraid, tired of waiting for the next bad surprise, tired of the past destroying her present and the people she cared about most. This time, no matter the consequences, she was taking control of the situation, going bravely out to meet it.

This time I'm going to resolve things, once and for all.

She shut off the TV and went upstairs. She stood beside Charlie's bed and gazed down at him, watching the deep rise and fall of his breathing, sadly studying the cuts and dark bruises across his face.

He and Val would probably never get together now. *And that's my fault, too. . . .*

"I'm so sorry, Charlie," she whispered.

She placed two pills beside his glass of water. She wondered if she'd ever see him again. Very gently she tucked the covers around his neck, then tiptoed from the room and closed the door behind her.

It only took a few minutes to collect her things—her coat and scarf, her gloves and her flashlight. She let herself out the back door and gasped sharply, ducking her head against the raw fury of the storm.

"Okay, Daniel," she murmured. "I'm the one you want. We belong together, you and I."

She took a deep breath, hunched her shoulders against the wind, and headed off through the snow to the house next door.

30

I must be lost. . . . How can I be lost?

Emma stumbled and nearly fell. She should have been there by now—it seemed hours since she'd climbed the fence—but the storm was so fierce, it left her with no sense of direction, no sense of time.

She stopped and struggled to catch her breath.

Her flashlight was useless out here—swearing bitterly, she pitched it out into the night. She put up one arm to shield her face, and then she turned in a slow, bewildered circle, unsure which way to go.

The world as she knew it was gone, faded and vanished beyond the swirling, silvery flakes of snow. The wind whipped about her, crying softly, and the air was pale, strangely translucent, as though she were trapped in a silent web of sleep.

And then, like a curtain slowly opening, the snow began to drift sideways, away from her . . .

And she saw him.

He was standing in the front doorway of the house, silhouetted against soft golden light. She could see his face, his windblown hair, and even from this distance, the glow of love in his dark, dark eyes. . . .

Emma's heart leaped within her.

Her body was trembling, and as she stood there at the bottom of the porch steps, she could feel his gaze caressing her, warming her, as though winter were only some distant dream.

"I'm here, Daniel," she said.

He made no move to approach her. His eyes were sad. His smile was brief and full of sorrow.

"You're so beautiful, Emma . . . so very beautiful. Just as I've always remembered."

Emma's heart ached within her. Silently she stared at him, and his tall, strong image shimmered for a moment through her tears.

"Every detail of your face . . . the sound of your voice . . . the sweetness of your smile." He hesitated, then said quietly, "You see, I've forgotten nothing. They're as much a part of me as my own heartbeat."

"Daniel . . . I . . ."

But she couldn't get the words out, and Daniel shook his head at her, his voice growing thick with emotion.

"I've missed you so much, Emma. If you only knew how much. When God took you away from me, he took my soul, as well."

"Please don't do this—"

"I've had no peace . . . no redemption. Death has been my everlasting torment." He faltered then, though his eyes remained steady upon her. "An endless journey of pain and regret. Always empty. Always searching."

Somehow Emma managed a nod. She closed the distance between them and slowly began to climb the steps.

"I know, Daniel—I've been searching, too. I realize that now."

She pondered for a moment, and the sadness in her smile matched his own.

"I've always felt like such a dreamer . . . so different from everyone else. I always hoped for this one perfect someone, only he never seemed to exist. And I never understood why, exactly, but now I do."

She paused on the top step. She held his gaze with her own.

"He was you," she whispered. "And I was waiting for you to find me."

Daniel stayed where he was. He didn't move, and he didn't reach for her, and the anguish in his eyes was almost more than she could bear.

"If you come through this door," he said softly, "you can never change your mind."

"I know."

"And there will be suffering. Suffering and pain I won't be able to protect you from."

She turned and stared out through the snow. She couldn't see her house anymore, or the fence, not the street or the sidewalk, or any part of the life that had been hers.

"I love you," she said.

"Then take my hand."

Emma did so, and stepped across the threshold.

31

❧∞ε

"*D*on't let go of me, Emma! We're almost there!"

Someone screaming . . . black waves of smoke . . . the groan and crash of collapsing timbers—

"*Hold tight to my hand!*"

And she realized he was dragging her, that he was crawling across the floor and pulling her with him, even as tongues of flame swept in at them from every side, licking up the walls of the barn and eating away at the overhead rafters. Blind and choking, Emma struggled to keep up, but there was so much smoke, so much blood, blood everywhere and she was soaked with it, her long skirts wet and red, Daniel's blood flowing and flowing as his grip on her began to loosen and the last of his strength drained away. . . .

"We're going to make it, Emma!" he promised. "I'm going to get you out of here!"

"I can't do it! I can't breathe—"

He clutched at her hand, slippery with blood, and she could feel something sliding from her finger. . . .

"Yes, you can!" Daniel cried. "There's a boarded-up window back here—it's big enough to crawl through, but it's high and you'll have to climb!"

"Then go! Go without me!"

"I'm going to boost you up! Emma, do you hear? Stay close to me—I have to knock out these boards and—"

His words were lost, drowned by a sudden roar of flames. As Emma screamed and rolled away, she felt the scorching heat, heard the deafening crash, and she saw him turn, for one brief instant she saw his eyes, the shock and the horror, the wild, infinite love as they gazed at her for the last time. And then the roof was caving in, everything collapsing around her, crushing her, burning her, burying her alive—

"*Daniel!*" she shrieked.

But Daniel didn't come—she couldn't see him—couldn't hear his voice, only the billowing blackness and the smell of burnt flesh—*my flesh!*—and the fading, the fading away. . . .

Oh, God—oh, God!—*something's wrong—it's not supposed to happen like this—it's supposed to be different this time—*

"Daniel!" she screamed again.

"*Emma!*"

She heard him then . . . the cry of a doomed soul. A second chance lost forever.

Through cracked and blistered lips, Emma tried once more to call his name, but there were no words anymore, no hope. *No pain . . . no struggle . . . no fear . . .*

Yet she could hear him, could still *hear* him, calling for her as he struggled back through the fire, as he fought his way through hell—

Oh, God . . . I'm dead. . . .

"No, Emma! Don't leave me!"

And she could see him now, too, as from a long way off, just as she could see herself, clutched tightly in the safety of his arms, pressed hard against the beating of his heart, shielded too late from the flames.

"It's no use, Daniel," she murmured. "We can't change what happened. . . ."

"Don't say that! I won't lose you again!"

"We can't change the past—we can't do over what's already been done."

"Oh, Emma, forgive me . . . forgive me. . . ."

Emma reached up gently for his face, but her hand seemed to pass right through him, through his skin blackened with smoke, through his eyes, glimmering with tears. And as Daniel pressed his lips against hers, the fire didn't matter anymore, nor the pain, nor the life that was sadly ending.

In the midst of tragedy, there was only love.

And suddenly Emma understood.

"Daniel," she whispered, "there's nothing to forgive. It wasn't your fault."

She heard him sob, a tortured cry that echoed across time and pierced her very soul.

"Don't you see?" she soothed him. "For whatever reason we don't understand, I wasn't meant to go with you that night, anymore than you were meant to stay. We have to accept that; we have to let it go. And you must forgive yourself."

She felt his tears upon her cheeks, his agony in her heart.

"How can I?" he wept. "Because of me, you died—"

"No . . . no . . . because of you, I *lived*! You gave me hope. You gave me the only happiness I ever knew. You gave me everything . . . *everything* . . . because you loved me so much."

Again she reached for his face; again her hand moved through him. She could see his tears, like tiny stars, and his eyes, as deep and black as endless midnight. And the air so thin, the smoke fading to shadows, and her words as fragile and final as a sigh . . .

"Promise me, Daniel . . ."

"Yes! Yes, I promise! Only don't leave me—please don't leave me alone!"

"I'll never leave you. I swear it. Not now. Not for all eternity."

And his kiss, the sweetest of memories . . . and all the years melting away . . .

Daniel! Where are you? What's happening!

"Shh . . . shh . . . It will all be over soon."

32

"Daniel . . . Daniel . . . what's happening . . ."

With a sudden gasp Emma jolted to consciousness.

She was lying on her back in the snow. A blast of ice stung her eyes, and her body felt numb and curiously detached. For several seconds she lay there, trying to figure out where she was, and then, very slowly, she pulled herself upright and stared at her surroundings.

It was still snowing heavily. The silvery night swirled around her, and there were no other sounds but the wind. She didn't recognize any familiar landmarks. There was no house, no porch, no open doorway.

No Daniel.

As Emma staggered to her feet, she was suddenly aware of a hazy light off in the distance, glowing eerily through the storm. For several moments she stood there, watching its strange flickering pattern, until realization finally began to dawn.

Something was burning.

The Farmington house was on fire.

Emma didn't move. Not when she heard the sirens screaming down the street. Not even when she heard the frantic shouts through the darkness as Charlie and Val came searching for her.

She simply stood there with tears in her eyes.

"You're free now," she whispered. "You're free."

33

"Well, what do you think of *that,* Sister! We were both of us perfectly *wrong!*"

Short Miss Loberg shook her head in dismay. She picked up her tea from the coffee table and took a long, reflective sip, oblivious to the scornful gaze of her sister.

"Wrong, indeed!" tall Miss Loberg sniffed. "Both of us were *not* wrong. *You* are the one who—"

"*I?*" short Miss Loberg broke in indignantly. "However do you figure that?"

"It doesn't matter," Emma broke in quickly, trying to make peace. "Really, it just doesn't matter anymore. What matters is that Daniel and Emma are together again, where they belong."

Tall Miss Loberg gave a snort. "Pity they had to burn the whole house down to do it! You'd think one fire would be quite enough."

"Yes . . . yes . . . you really would." Short Miss Loberg leaned over and patted Emma's arm consolingly. "Well, at least you didn't have to die, dear. I'm very glad of that."

"We couldn't have come to your funeral, anyway," the taller sister added. "We've been snowed in all week."

Emma gave an amused nod. Beside her on the loveseat, Charlie was trying to master a china cup and saucer with his one good arm. She nudged him slyly in the ribs with her elbow, and the teacup teetered precariously.

"Well, I might have died out in that snowstorm if Charlie hadn't found me," she admitted.

The two sisters beamed at Charlie, who squirmed uncomfortably.

"We're so very glad you came to visit, Charlie," short Miss Loberg insisted. "What a treat for the two of us!"

The two women stared at him. Charlie squirmed again. He tried to smile politely around a bite of macaroon.

"We're just on our way to see his doctor," Emma explained. "That's why we can't stay long. We just wanted you to know what happened."

"Poor Charlie!" Short Miss Loberg sighed. "And how did you break that shoulder of yours? Are you in much pain?"

The taller Miss Loberg cast her a withering glance. "Oh, for heaven's sake, Sister—of course he's in pain! You can just look at his face and tell how he's suffering!"

"But he's being so very brave about it, don't you think?"

"Of course he's being brave!" Tall Miss Loberg

rolled her eyes. "Men never talk about pain! In our day it was pain and battle scars—and—and female conquests, of course—these were the things that built a man's character! Isn't that right, Charlie?"

"Oh, Charlie has a *lot* of character," Emma agreed.

Charlie's face went beet red. He shot Emma a murderous look, and she grinned back at him.

"Why, Charlie, I believe you need a refill," short Miss Loberg said, suddenly flustered. "Let me make a fresh pot." She paused in the kitchen doorway and added, "Sister, why don't you get Charlie some more cookies?"

Tall Miss Loberg didn't move. She was staring at Charlie with an odd smile.

"You're perfectly capable of finding the cookies on your own," she said.

"But I'd much rather have your help," the other firmly replied.

Tall Miss Loberg pinched her lips together. She stood up and marched menacingly into the kitchen.

"I told you," Emma said, choking back a laugh.

"Can we just get out of here?" Charlie muttered. "Told me what?"

"They're competing for you. They think you're a stud."

"Oh, shut up, Emma."

Emma stared at him. She watched him for a long, thoughtful moment, and an unexpected surge of emotion went through her.

"Thanks, Charlie."

"For what?" he grumbled.

"For being there through all this. For not giving up

on me. For coming to find me the other night."

"For not having you committed," he finished dryly.

"Okay, that, too. But I *had* to go to Daniel, you know that. I had to do something to help him, to end it once and for all. And I just . . ."

Her voice trailed away. Had it really been only a week since she'd returned to the Farmington house? Seen Daniel for the very last time? Only a week, yet it was already beginning to seem like a dream. . . .

"And I just . . ."

Again she trailed off. Charlie put his saucer clumsily down on the table.

"You felt responsible for me getting hurt," he mumbled. "I know that."

"You do?"

"Of course I do. That night before you left, you stood by my bed and said you were sorry."

"I thought you were asleep."

"I was . . . almost. But for just a second your thoughts got through to me, and I knew I had to find you."

Emma's face grew pensive. "And that's when Val came back?"

"She said she couldn't see to drive—she couldn't even get her wipers to work." Charlie glanced sideways at his sister. "And she said she had a feeling you were gonna do something really stupid."

"She said that?"

"You're so transparent, Em."

"Hmmm." Emma grew silent. She stared down at the coffee table until Charlie leaned over and jostled her.

"She's a good friend, you know."

"I know. The best."

"If it hadn't been for her, I'd never have made it out there to find you. I was so strung out on those pills. I couldn't get into your mind to find out what was going on, and I was . . ."

He stopped and took a deep breath. His voice was low and solemn. "I was so scared. I was so scared you were dead."

For a long moment there was silence. Emma's eyes filled with tears, and she quickly blinked them away.

It was Charlie who finally spoke.

"But"– he sighed–"no such luck."

"You are such a jerk!"

Her brother hid a smile. "And for what it's worth," he added, "I'm really glad you and Val talked and straightened things out."

"I shouldn't have said what I did to her . . . about the bet and all. God, it was *horrible* of me! But I was so upset, and it just slipped out. I was sure I'd ruined things between you two."

"Just let me worry about that, okay? I can take care of myself." Charlie thought a moment. "And Val."

Emma drew back, fixing him with a mock frown. "Well, *someone's* pretty sure of himself, I think!"

"Just do me one favor," Charlie said. "Promise me you two won't talk about . . . you know . . . *everything.*"

"But the *everythings* are the best part." Emma smiled at him sweetly. "*Especially* when they're about you."

"Well, here we are!" short Miss Loberg announced as the two sisters came back into the room. After replenishing tea and cookies all around, they settled in again for the rest of the story.

"There's really not much more to tell," Emma said.

She'd felt obligated to let the sisters know that the drama was finally over, but she and Charlie had both agreed to a very condensed version of that fateful night's events. Now there was only one more thing Emma wanted to do.

"Here," she told them. "I want you to have this."

Reaching into her pocket, she pulled out a ring—a thin gold band with a heart in its center.

"But that's Emma Farmington's ring!" short Miss Loberg exclaimed. "Whyever would you want to give it up?"

"Because I don't—*she* doesn't—need it anymore," Emma corrected herself. "You thought the ring had survived with Emma. But the truth is, it slipped off her finger in the fire."

As the shorter Miss Loberg passed the ring to her sister, she asked, "So how did you find it in the first place?"

"I don't know," Emma admitted. "We'll probably never know. Maybe it came off in Daniel's hand. Or Betsey found it later in the ashes after the barn burned down. And somehow it ended up back in the house after all those years."

Emma sat back against the cushions. She felt curiously light, as though a huge weight had been lifted at last.

"Anyway, I thought you'd like to keep it. Maybe put it away in Emma's box."

Short Miss Loberg nodded. Her eyes grew moist and she squeezed Emma's hand. "Thank you, my dear. What a lovely treasure. Isn't it a lovely treasure, Sister?"

Tall Miss Loberg didn't answer. Her cheeks were

unusually pink, and she was fussing at the lace on her collar.

"Sister?" Short Miss Loberg frowned. "Are you all right?"

"Perfectly all right!" her sister snapped. "Don't I look all right?"

Puzzled, Emma glanced over at Charlie. She was just in time to see him wink at tall Miss Loberg.

"We have to go," Emma said, and immediately stood up. "I wouldn't want poor, helpless Charlie to be late."

After promises to come again for tea, Emma and Charlie started down the walkway to their car. Emma glanced back to make sure the sisters weren't watching, then promptly punched Charlie on his good arm.

"Ouch! What was that for?"

"Shame on you!" Emma scolded. "What did you think you were doing in there?"

Charlie looked down at her, deadpan. "Well, I just thought if Val changed her mind about the dance, I could ask that tall sister to go with me. I bet she was a knockout when she was younger."

"You are so bad."

"I'm serious!"

"Get in the car."

It took several minutes for the engine to warm up. As Emma wiped one mitten across the windshield, she was startled to hear Charlie's sudden question.

"Do you miss him?" he asked quietly.

"Miss who?"

"You know who, and you have to talk about it sometime."

Emma rested her hands on the steering wheel and drew a huge sigh. She leaned back in the seat and closed her eyes. "I miss the way he loved me. I miss the way I was special to him."

She opened her eyes again. She looked over at Charlie, but he seemed deep in thought.

"But I know Daniel's at peace now," Emma went on slowly. "I know he's with Emma. And I know I had something to do with making him so happy."

Charlie's nod was almost imperceptible. "You make a lot of people happy, Em."

"I do?"

"Well, not me, but yeah, a lot of people."

Grinning, he reached over and ruffled her hair. "Don't worry, it'll happen."

"What will? You moving far, far away?"

"You'll end up with some really great guy," Charlie went on, ignoring her. "Maybe even almost as great as I am. You know, someone you'll adore and worship, like Val does me."

Emma revved the engine. She headed the car down the street, and then she smiled.

"Not in this lifetime," she said.

ABOUT THE AUTHOR

Richie Tankersley Cusick is the author of more than twenty books for young adults, in addition to several adult novels. She lives with her cocker spaniel Meg outside Kansas City, where she is currently at work on her next novel.